DEATH GRIP

Suddenly Nate had a 50-pound bundle of raw ferocity in his arms. He flung his free hand in front of his face and nearly cried out when the wolverine's iron jaws clamped down. Tottering under an onslaught of claws and teeth, he tripped over his own feet and wound up on his back.

Nate had to drop the tomahawk so he could grab hold of the animal's throat as it hurled itself at his face. Muscles straining, he held the enraged predator at bay with one arm while he deflected its rapier claws with his other forearm. Locked together, they rolled to the right, then to the left.

The only weapon Nate had left was his butcher knife, but to reach it he had to lower one of his arms. Taking a gamble, he swooped his left hand to his waist. His fingers closed on the beaded sheath—but the knife was gone! In the flurry of combat it had fallen out!

Before Nate could lift his arm again, the wolverine gave a terrific wrench of its whole body and broke free of his grasp. Its mouth opened wide and swept to his exposed throat. He felt its teeth on his skin.

He was going to die!

22
WILDERNESS

Trail's End
David Thompson

LEISURE BOOKS **NEW YORK CITY**

Dedicated to Judy, Joshua, and Shane.

A LEISURE BOOK®

October 1995

Published by

Dorchester Publishing Co., Inc.
276 Fifth Avenue
New York, NY 10001

Printed in the United States of America.

Chapter One

Nate King reined up the instant the forest fell silent.

A moment before, the big free trapper had been winding up a steep switchback toward a jagged ridge. He rode easily in the saddle, as befitted a man who spent so much of his time on horseback.

Like many of his hardy breed, the mountain man favored an Indian style of dress. Buckskins covered his powerful frame. Moccasins protected his feet. On his head rested a dark beaver hat crowned by a single eagle feather.

Whenever Nate ventured from his family's cabin nestled high in the majestic Rocky Mountains, he went armed for bear, as the saying had it. In this instance a brace of flintlock pistols were wedged under his wide brown leather belt. On his right hip hung a long butcher knife in a beaded sheath. On his left side was a Shoshone tomahawk. An ammo pouch, powder horn, and

5

David Thompson

possibles bag were all slanted across his broad chest. And held firmly in his left hand with the polished stock braced on his thigh was a Hawken rifle.

Moments ago the surrounding slopes had been alive with sounds: the gay chirping of sparrows, the strident squawk of jays, the chattering of squirrels, and more. Then, as abruptly as if a gigantic invisible hand had smothered every living creature, the sounds had died.

Now the air lay deathly still. Nate King cocked his ruggedly handsome head from side to side, but detected no hint of noise other than the fluttering whisper of the northwesterly breeze. Yet there had to be something—or someone—out there.

Small animals were notoriously skittish. The cough of a roving grizzly, the throaty growl of a prowling painter, or the passage of a large body of men would quiet all wildlife within earshot.

Nate, though, had not heard a thing, and years of living in the high country had heightened his senses to where they were keener than those of most men.

The big trapper shifted to scan a tract of firs above him and dense pines to his right. Not so much as a chickadee stirred, that he could see. Which in itself meant little.

Predators and hostiles were not about to advertise their presence. The first inkling there might be of an attack could well be the roar of an onrushing silver tip or the searing jolt of an arrow in the ribs. He had to stay alert.

Trappers did not last long if they were careless. In recent years, hundreds of young men had flocked to the frontier to make their living at the fur trade, and many scores of them would never see their kin back in the States ever again.

Bleached bones were all that remained of their youthful dreams, their craving for adventure.

Tense moments dragged by. Nate rested his thumb on the hammer of his rifle and lightly touched his finger to the trigger. His black stallion was gazing to the northwest with its ears pricked. He looked in the same direction but saw nothing out of the ordinary.

Ever so gradually, the woodland resumed its natural rhythm as if the gigantic hand that had been smothering everything had been lifted so the creatures could breathe again. Birds sang. Squirrels scampered about on lofty branches. Chipmunks did the same over boulders and logs.

Nate let himself relax. The danger had passed. He could go on about his business. Bending to the right, he fixed his piercing green eyes on the ground while nudging the stallion onward with a jab of both heels.

Tracks were few and far between, but there were enough for the seasoned mountaineer to keep from losing the trail. Complete prints showed five toes, although the smallest barely left an impression. Claws were also evident.

Less experienced trappers might have mistaken the tracks for those of a wolf. But Nate knew better. Wolves only had four toes, and their pads were shaped differently. The prints he followed had been made by a creature much more fierce, a creature shunned by Indians and whites alike.

Nate King was after an animal which, pound for pound, was rated the most powerful of any its size. Its reputation for savagery was unrivaled even by grizzlies. It would eat anything it could catch and kill, as well as carrion.

Early French trappers had a name for the animal, "carcajou," which was still used by some mountaineers. A few of Nate's acquaintances had taken to referring to the voracious brutes as "gluttons," based on the habit the creatures had of gorging themselves to the point of stupor. The majority, however, simply used the name the creatures were known by east of the Mississippi: wolverines.

For several weeks now, a particularly vicious specimen had been plaguing Nate's family with repeated visits. At first it had only shown an interest in the many ducks and geese that routinely flocked to a small lake near the remote King homestead. His young son, Zach, had found the first clues, in the form of three ducks that had been literally ripped to shreds and a couple of clear tracks in the blood-soaked mud at the water's edge.

Nate had not been overly alarmed by the report. Wolverines, by and large, tended to fight shy of human beings. He'd assumed the beast would tire of lying in wait for water fowl and wander elsewhere. But as the days turned to weeks and the weeks became a full month, he'd grown increasingly concerned.

The wolverine had started to rove closer to the King cabin. Nate had stumbled on tracks close to the trail his wife and infant daughter took daily down to the water's edge. The animal, quite obviously, had been spying on them. He began to worry that perhaps it had designs on tiny Evelyn, as wolverines were known to be fond of fawns and other young animals.

Then the beast had developed the habit of circling the cabin late at night. Its pungent scent always spooked their horses, and the animals would prance and snort and whinny until Nate appeared to soothe them. On a half-dozen occasions he'd heard the wolverine off in the thick brush, growling and snarling as if in frustration that it could not get at the stock because of the small corral in which he kept them penned.

The final straw had been an incident the previous night.

Nate had been snuggled against the warm form of his lovely Shoshone wife, Winona, in the pine bed he had fashioned with his own two hands. Close by, stretched out on a buffalo robe in front of the stone fireplace, slept their son. Little Evelyn had been snug in her small cradle.

The cabin had been cozy and warm and tranquil.

Suddenly a tremendous uproar had erupted outside. The horses had been nickering and stomping in abject fright.

Nate had grabbed his Hawken and dashed into the darkness in his bare feet. He'd rushed to the south side of the cabin just in time to see a long, hairy form trying to force its muscular bulk between two of the rails to get at a terrified colt his wife's mare had given birth to months ago.

Out of sheer reflex, Nate had whipped the Hawken to his shoulder, fixed a hasty bead, and fired. In his sluggish state he'd missed. The ball gouged into the rail inches from the wolverine's head.

Like a streak of lightning, the scourge of the Rockies had whirled and vanished in the undergrowth.

Nate had automatically reached for his powder horn to reload and only then realized that he had left it and everything else he needed inside. Fortunately for him, his wife and son arrived, both bearing their own rifles.

"Was it the glutton, Pa?" Zach had asked.

"Sure was," Nate had confirmed.

The boy had taken a few eager steps. "Reckon we should go after it before the varmint gets away?"

Winona had glanced sharply at Nate. There had been no need for her to say a word, because they both had been thinking the same thing: It would have been foolhardy to dash into the inky forest where the wolverine was in its element. "No, son," Nate had answered. "We'd best stick close to the cabin in case it tries to get at the horses again."

Thankfully, the rest of the night had proven uneventful. At first light, Nate had thrown a blanket and his saddle on the stallion, added a parfleche laden with pemmican and jerky which his wife had thoughtfully prepared, and headed out to track the troublemaker down no matter how long it took.

To Nate's surprise, he'd located the animal's tracks with little difficulty. Now, after spending the greater part of the morning on its trail, he felt that he was drawing near his quarry.

Strangely enough, the wolverine did not appear to be in any hurry. It had traveled upward at a leisurely pace, meandering as its heart desired.

Nate had counted on finding where the creature had holed up for the day, but so far the voracious beast had given no indication that it intended to stop anytime soon. He gained the crest of the switchback and reined up to survey the ridge. The tracks led straight across.

Tightly clustered lodgepole pines covered the facing slope. The trees were so jammed together that the stallion would not be able to go faster than a brisk walk. He would fall behind his wily adversary, but it couldn't be helped. If he circled around, he risked losing the trail.

Cradling the Hawken in the crook of his left elbow, Nate trotted to the tree line. Scant sunlight penetrated the upper terrace, resulting in perpetual shadow at ground level.

Slightly uneasy, Nate warily advanced. He chided himself for letting the gloom get to him. Or was it something else? he wondered. A vague feeling came over him that he was being watched. Try as he might, though, he failed to catch sight of the glutton or any other animal that might account for it.

Men who lived in the wilderness long enough learned not to discount their intuition. Many a trapper had his gut instincts to thank for saving his hide from lurking hostiles or wild beasts.

The tall boles of the lodgepoles hemmed Nate in on all sides. He had to pick his way with care. Often the stallion squeezed through gaps where there was barely space to spare. On several occasions Nate had to lift his legs and fork them over the saddle so they wouldn't scrape against trunks.

All the while, the mountain man climbed higher. Having to constantly glance up to insure the carcajou wasn't lying in wait above him put a crick in his neck.

The tracks were harder to find thanks to a spongy layer of pine needles covering the forest floor. Even the stallion barely left prints.

Presently Nate had to dismount and bend low in order not to lose the trail. The minutes passed slowly. Off to the north, a red hawk screeched. To the southwest a coyote yipped, a rarity during daylight hours.

So engrossed did Nate become in his task that he didn't realize he had reached the end of the lodgepole growth until he almost bumped into a boulder in his path. Straightening, he discovered a twisted outcropping of solid rock dotted with many more boulders. The tracks went on into the maze.

Nate hesitated. Taking the horse in there was out of the question. He was reluctant to go on without it, yet he had no choice. Tying the reins to a pine, he hefted the Hawken, thumbed back the hammer, and cat-footed around a boulder half the size of his cabin.

Clearly imbedded in the bare earth were the wolverine's prints. The animal had been moving rapidly, as if it were suddenly in a hurry to get somewhere, leading Nate to conclude that it had a den nearby.

Before going around obstacles, Nate always took a peek first. All too vividly, he recollected the time he had tracked a black bear into some rocks and nearly been torn apart when the bear came at him from out of nowhere. He wasn't about to make the same mistake twice.

Here in the outcropping, the air was totally still. Sounds were amplified, so Nate had to be vigilant to avoid making any. He stepped over all dry twigs and patches of loose gravel.

Unexpectedly, up ahead, a bird twittered shrilly. The cry was strangled off, as if its throat had been torn asunder or its neck broken. Then a series of low rumbling growls echoed off the boulders and rock walls.

Leveling the Hawken and keeping his trigger finger tensed to fire, Nate edged around a jutting spike of stone. Before him was a narrow path, which shortly ended at an oval cleared space about five feet in diameter. In the very center lay a dozen bloody gray feathers.

Nate examined them. He nearly stepped on a tiny dark eyeball, which had been severed from the bird's head. Fresh wolverine tracks took him to a path that angled to the southwest. He went a single step and froze when a menacing snarl rose from seemingly close at hand.

Pivoting on a heel, Nate sought the source. The high boulders and rock walls had distorted the sound so badly that the was unable to pinpoint the glutton's position. But something told him the creature knew exactly where he was. Either it had somehow caught his scent, or it had heard him.

Firming his grip on the rifle, Nate inched forward. He paused after each stride. More feathers littered the ground. When he rounded a bend, he found the bird's head, partially eaten.

Nate recognized it as having been a gray jay, or Whiskey Jack, as some of the trappers called them. A little further on, he came upon a single gnawed leg and several long, black tail feathers.

The path looped this way and that, never running in a straight line for more than a dozen feet. Nate was glad when he stepped out into the open on the rim of a barren slope. He scoured the area below him, but didn't spot the carcajou. A check of the ground at his feet told him why.

The wolverine had not descended. Instead, it had slanted to the left and made off along the edge of the outcropping.

Nate gave chase. Since the beast knew he was after it, stealth was no longer essential. He poured on the speed, running flat out, and when he came to where the wolverine had skirted the southwest corner and headed due east again, a stab of anxiety speared through him.

The glutton was doubling back on itself! It was heading for the stallion!

Fairly flying, Nate flashed past boulder after boulder. He doubted the wolverine could bring down a full grown horse, but it might cripple the black so severely that he would have to put the horse out of its misery, leaving him stranded, afoot, many miles from home.

A towering boulder loomed before him. Nate started to swing around it, but stopped cold in his tracks on glimpsing a streak of motion in smaller boulders beyond. Tucking the polished rifle stock to his shoulder, he stood perfectly still and waited for the beast to show itself again.

There was a faint scraping noise, such as claws might make on stone, followed by unnerving silence.

Nate took a few short steps. He needed to lure the carcajou into the open, and to that end he extended his left arm and ran his fingernails over the rough surface of the boulder. He hoped the scratching would excite the wolverine's curiosity and it would pop into sight just long enough for him to squeeze the trigger. That was all he asked. One clear shot.

Nothing happened.

Keeping his back to the tall boulder, Nate glided along its base. His attention was turned low to the ground, where the glutton was most likely to appear.

Wolverines were not large animals. Males seldom measured more than four feet long or weighed more than 50 pounds. But every square inch of their compact frames was packed with steely sinews. And their long claws and tapered teeth made formidable weapons.

So intent was Nate on the area around the smaller boulders that he neglected to pay attention to anything above the level of his waist. Almost too late, he registered a hint of something dark brown at shoulder height and snapped his head up to see the wolverine spring from a rock shelf.

It all happened so incredibly fast.

Nate already had the Hawken raised. He spun and tried to bring the gun to bear, but the carcajou was on him in the blink of an eye. The bruising impact staggered him backward and caused his finger to curl around the trigger. His rifle belched smoke and lead.

Teeth slashed at Nate's forearm, missing by a whisker as he stumbled against the tall boulder. Automatically he lashed out, driving the stock at the wolverine's head. The beast danced aside with astounding ease, snaked in close, and bit into the fringe on Nate's leggings. He winced as those razor teeth sheared through buckskin and flesh.

Wrenching to the right, Nate swung the Hawken as he might a club. Again the hissing wolverine evaded the blow. In leaping to the right to get out of reach of its wicked teeth, Nate neglected to note a small boulder. He tripped and fell, jarring his spine when he crashed onto his back.

Snarling in feral fury, the wolverine was quick to seize the advantage. It leaped.

The only thing that saved Nate from having his throat torn wide open was the Hawken. By a sheer fluke, he brought the rifle up at the selfsame moment that the glutton's jaws lanced at his jugular. The brute's teeth crunched on the barrel rather than his vulnerable neck.

Hot, fetid breath blew over Nate's face as he heaved with all his strength. He partially dislodged the wolverine. Its claws cut into his shirt, shredding the buckskin as if it were so much wet paper. He twisted and rolled onto one knee, still holding onto the rifle.

The wolverine also held on. Digging in its oversized paws, it yanked on the barrel.

Nate let go. The predator was thrown off balance by its own momentum, giving him the fleeting chance he needed to make a grab for the flintlocks wedged under his belt. As the right one cleared the top of the belt, the carcajou released the Hawken and darted in close, its glistening teeth poised above his shin. He jerked his leg out of harm's way, then fired. His rushed shot went wide by a hand's width, plowing into the hard earth instead.

Most animals would have bolted after the first shot, let alone the second. Not the wolverine. Fear was not part of its nature. Its kind had been known to tangle with grizzlies and panthers, if they dared cross its path. Mountain men and Indians alike had witnessed wolverines drive both from prey that was rightfully theirs.

So it was no surprise that the blasts of the rifle and the smoothbore pistol had no effect. The wolverine coiled, then, apparently mistaking the smoking flintlock for an appendage of its two-legged foe, bit at the tip of the smoking barrel.

Nate drew his other pistol, pointed it at the glutton's chest, and fired at so close a range that the beast was singed by powder burns. The .55-caliber flintlock packed quite a wallop, sufficient to knock a man down at 20 yards, yet it hardly slowed the wolverine. Snarling viciously, the carcajou closed in.

Back-pedaling, Nate hurled the spent pistols at the creature's head. It dodged aside, allowing him to drop a hand to his tomahawk. Arcing the weapon overhead, he drove the keen edge at the wolverine's skull.

The carcajou's lightning reflexes came to its rescue one more time. The tomahawk swished by its cheek. Whirling, the wolverine lunged at the trapper's wrist.

A desperate yank of his arm saved Nate from losing his hand. He swung again and again, but couldn't connect.

Wiry as a cat and as elusive as a phantom, the glutton was next to impossible to hit. Nate aimed high. He aimed low. He fought with all the skill at his command, yet it wasn't enough. The wolverine kept one step ahead of him.

They continually circled one another, each seeking an opening that would end the fray. Nate thought he saw one when the wolverine snapped at his leg, missed, and slipped as it threw itself backward out of harm's way. He took a short step and drove the tomahawk at its neck. By rights, he should have separated the head from the bearish body. But the thing was too quick for him, and before the tomahawk could connect, it vaulted upward, ramming into his chest.

Suddenly Nate had a 50-pound bundle of raw ferocity in his arms. He flung his free hand in front of his face and nearly cried out when those iron jaws clamped down. Tottering under an onslaught of claws and teeth, he tripped over his own feet and wound up on his back, like before.

Nate had to drop the tomahawk so he could grab hold of the carcajou's throat as it hurled itself at his face. Muscles straining, he held the enraged predator at bay with one arm while he deflected its rapier claws with his other forearm. Locked together, they rolled to the right, then to the left.

The beast had a pungent body odor and foul breath. Nate could scarcely stand to inhale. He shoved with all his might, but the wolverine clung to him, its claws digging deep. A moist sensation crept along his arms and down over his chest.

David Thompson

Nate knew that he couldn't hold the glutton at bay for long. Unless he broke free, he would weaken from loss of blood and it would finish him off.

The only weapon he had left was his butcher knife, but to reach it he had to lower one of his arms. Taking a gamble, he swooped his left hand to his waist. His fingers closed on the beaded sheath—but the knife was gone! In the flurry of combat it had fallen out!

Before Nate could lift his arm again, the wolverine gave a terrific wrench of its whole body and broke free of his grasp. Its mouth opened wide and swept to his exposed throat. He felt its teeth on his skin.

He was going to die!

Chapter Two

Time stood still.

To Nate King it seemed as if an eternity went by, when in reality it was no more than five intensely horrifying seconds. Awful, harrowing moments in which he braced for the searing pain that would rack him when the creature's teeth ripped through his soft flesh.

Yet there was no pain, no agonizing spasm, nothing except the light prick of deadly teeth pressed almost gently against his skin. Gradually it dawned on Nate that the wolverine had stopped moving. It had sagged against him, then gone limp.

Gingerly, Nate reached up and pried the glutton's jaws wide enough to ease them off his neck. Shoving the animal to one side, he swiftly scrambled erect. A few feet away lay his tomahawk, which he scooped up and elevated to strike.

The battle was over. The wolverine posed no

further threat. Evidently the pistol shot had struck a vital organ, but the carcajou had fought on until it expired. Blood oozed from the entry hole and was forming a scarlet puddle.

Nate reclaimed his weapons, stepped over to the big boulder, and wearily sank down. Leaning back, he stared at the bestial terror and marveled at his narrow escape.

Wolverines, like grizzlies, were notoriously hard to kill. Or, as the members of the trapping fraternity liked to phrase it, they were "powerful hard to die."

No less a personage than Meriwether Lewis had first applied the saying after the men on the famed Lewis and Clark expedition encountered a few grizzlies and nearly lost their lives. One bear, in particular, had been shot eight times through its vital parts and still would not go down.

Gluttons were no less formidable. They would fight on even when mortally stricken, as the one before Nate had done. He made a mental note to fight shy of its kin in the future unless he had no other choice.

While Nate rested, he reloaded the spent flintlocks and the Hawken. It annoyed him that his hands shook a little at first, but they steadied after his blood stopped racing in his veins.

As any hunter worthy of the name knew, it was a cardinal sin to let any part of a slain animal go to waste. With that in mind, Nate drew his butcher knife and returned to the body.

Skinning the beast took less than half an hour. Nate hauled it away from the puddle, then hunkered and rolled the wolverine over. His next step was to slit the hide open down the back of each hind leg. Gripping the edge of the pelt in one hand, he slowly peeled it down over the body, cutting ligaments and muscles as it was necessary and always remembering to hold the edge angled toward the carcass.

Since Winona was much better at curing hides than he was, Nate opted to leave that chore for her. But he did take a step to insure the pelt would stay in prime shape. Using the tomahawk, he split the skull open. He had to pry a bit with his knife before he could slip his fingers into the cranial cavity and remove the brain, which he rubbed over the underside of the hide as he might a sponge. When the whole pelt had been so treated, he tossed what remained of the brain to the ground, rolled up the hide, and was ready to go.

Nate strolled back to the stallion. After the ordeal he had just been through, it felt grand to breathe in the crisp mountain air and to smell the fragrant scent of pine and the musty odor of the rich soil.

He tied the hide on the stallion, forked leather, and turned the big black eastward. At a brisk trot he descended the mountain. On reaching the level valley floor, he goaded his mount into a distance-eating canter.

Nate was eager to get home. He spent so much time away from his family during the fall and spring trapping seasons that the days spent with them were precious to him.

It was a glorious afternoon, with the sky as blue as a deep lake and the verdant valley lush with grass and flowers. Wildlife was abundant; deer grazed unafraid in the open, shaggy mountain buffalo hunted the valley's fringe, bald eagles soared high on the air currents, while everywhere frolicked birds and lesser animals.

The Rocky Mountains, Nate frequently mused, were the next best thing to paradise on earth.

David Thompson

Among the pristine peaks and winding valleys a man could live as he pleased, accountable to no one except his Maker. Here a man enjoyed true freedom, a state those living east of the broad Mississippi could no longer claim as their birthright.

It saddened Nate to think of how far the country had fallen in so short a time. Having lived in New York City until his eighteenth year, he had seen for himself how politicians and lawyers had taken the basic tenets outlined in the Constitution and perverted them for their own ends.

With his own eyes, Nate had read where journalists referred to the Government as if it were a holy entity with the God-given right to rule the people as those who were in Government saw fit. Such profound ignorance would one day do the country irreparable harm.

Among the half-dozen or so books lining a short shelf in the King cabin was one dealing with the works of Thomas Paine, whose sentiments Nate shared. The firebrand of liberty during the American Revolution had once written: "When extraordinary power and extraordinary pay are allotted to any individual in Government, he becomes the center round which every kind of corruption generates and forms." Paine had referred to such power mongers as "parasites," and Nate wholeheartedly agreed.

In the Rocky Mountains there were no parasites, because there was no government. Men and women, red and white, lived as they pleased. They did as they wanted, when they wanted, and woe to the fool who claimed they couldn't. Anyone who took on airs paid for his idiocy at the point of a gun, if need be.

Nate would no more give up his life in the high country than he would his arms and legs. True freedom, he had learned, was a greater treasure than gold, more desirable than diamonds. The person who had it had everything. The person who lacked it lived in an invisible prison of someone else's making.

Such were the thoughts that occupied the free trapper as he made his way toward home and hearth. Preoccupied as he was, he almost missed spotting the fresh horse tracks he came upon when still several miles from his cabin.

Drawing rein in alarm, Nate studied them closely. He counted nine riders, all tolled. None of their mounts had been shod, which indicated they were Indians. And they were heading in the same direction he was.

Nate urgently brought the black stallion to a gallop. Nine warriors were too many for a simple hunting party; it must be a war party. There was an outside chance they were Shoshones, his adopted people. But they might also be Blackfeet or Piegans or Utes, hostiles who would extermin-ate his family without a second thought.

Filled with fear for those he loved, Nathaniel King sped like the wind on down the valley, his ears straining to hear the war whoops he prayed would not shatter the serenity of his mountain retreat.

Once, years ago, a major by the name of Stephen Long had been commissioned by the United States Government to survey a portion of the vast unknown western stretches with an eye to finding the source of the Arkansas, Red and Platte Rivers.

Long ran into some problems. He had a hard time telling which river was which. He never found the source of the Arkansas and wrongly thought the Canadian River was the Red River.

David Thompson

The major's confusion was not limited to waterways. On reaching the Rockies, he mistook a high peak for the one previously discovered by Zebulon Pike, even though Pike's Peak was far to the south.

On his return to civilization, Long produced a map of his travels, which became the standard for many years to come. On it, he labeled the prairie as the "Great American Desert" and compared it to the immense sandy deserts of Africa. The plains were, in his opinion, "uninhabitable by a people depending on agriculture."

The peak he 'discovered' became known among the mountaineers as Long's Peak, and it was north of there, in a picturesque lateral valley ridged by lofty mountains and dominated by a beautiful lake, that Nate King had settled.

The cabin was not his originally. Nate's uncle had built it and had intended to set down roots, but a vengeful Ute had made wolf meat of Ezekiel.

Since taking it over, Nate had made many improvements. Among them were genuine glass windows. Imported from the States at great cost and brought in on a caravan from St. Louis, they were the talk of the trapping fraternity.

Most free trappers either lived with Indians or lived Indian-fashion in lodges or dugouts they abandoned at the end of each winter. Few went to all the bother Zeke had done in erecting a sturdy cabin. And none had gone to the lengths of Nate King in improving their cabin to where it resembled an ordinary home.

At the annual rendezvous, Nate's peers were not above ribbing him about his homestead. They sincerely thought it strange that he would go to so much bother. And they weren't the only ones. Nate's wife thought it strange, too.

Trail's End

Winona King had never quite become accustomed to living in a cabin. Having been reared in a succession of buffalo hide tepees, she had been absolutely flabbergasted when her new husband had proposed they move into the "wooden lodge."

She could still remember that first day, over 12 winters ago, when she had spent all of an afternoon wandering around in a daze, running her hands over the smooth logs and the stone fireplace and the floor and the furniture.

It had amazed her that her husband did not desire a lodge that could be taken down and transported to new sites as the need arose.

Her people, the Shoshones, migrated over a wide area throughout the year, and it had taken considerable adjustment on her part to accept Nate's plan to stay in one place not only for an entire winter, but for the *rest of their lives*. Secretly, she had wondered if perhaps he was in his right mind.

Now she was grateful to him.

Winona stood at the long counter Nate had built, chopping roots she planned to add to the soup she was making for their supper, and grinned as she stared out the window at her son.

It was nice having the glass. The pane kept out dust and bugs, yet let them see what was taking place outdoors.

And it was nice having solid walls instead of hides, which constantly had to be mended or replaced.

Likewise, Winona appreciated having the stone fireplace. It kept the cabin much warmer during the coldest weather than the fire in a hide lodge ever had.

Winona gazed over a shoulder at her infant daughter, who rested quietly in a cradleboard, and smiled. "I guess I am fortunate to have a husband who goes to so much trouble for us, little one," she said in impeccable English.

Evelyn cooed and gurgled.

It had taken many moons for Winona to master the white tongue, and she was rightfully proud of her accomplishment. Nate liked to brag that she spoke English better than he did. If that was true, she had him to thank, for he had spent many days and nights teaching her.

Through the window, Winona could see her son busy making arrows. He owned a rifle and pistol and he was a crack shot, but long ago Nate had decided that they should ration their ammunition as much as possible by using traditional Shoshone weapons when they hunted close to home.

Their safety was an added consideration. The sound of a shot could carry for miles in the rarified air at higher elevations, and if heard by a roving war party would draw them like a flame drew moths. By using quieter weapons, they eliminated that risk.

Winona finished chopping the last root, set down the knife, and wiped her hands on a cloth towel. Taking the cradleboard, she walked out into the bright sunlight.

"How soon do you reckon Pa will be back, Ma?" young Zachary King interrupted his work to ask.

"Before the sun sets," Winona said, remembering the promise Nate had given her. Squatting, she slid the wide straps attached to the sides of the cradleboard over her arms so that the cradleboard rested against her back. From a bench by the door she took a wooden pail "Care to join us?"

"Sure," Zach replied, glad to have an excuse to stretch his legs. He had been working on arrows since noon and needed a break. As he rose he thought of his rifle in the cabin but decided not to fetch it. They were only going to the lake, and he had his pistol.

The well-worn trail wound through pines to the water's edge. As usual, plenty of ducks, geese and brants were in evidence. Overhead, gulls wheeled and squawked.

This was the second trip Winona had made that day. Needing water for the soup, she knelt and dipped the pail in.

Runoff from the ring of adjacent peaks fed the lake. Year round the water was ice cold and so clear that a person on the shore could see the bottom a dozen yards out. Winona spied a school of small fish being shadowed by a larger one.

Zach moved a few feet off and idly regarded the forest to the west. He had something on his mind that he was reluctant to bring up, so rather than get right to the point, he approached the subject in a roundabout manner. "I've been meaning to ask you a question," he commented as casually as he could.

"Which is?" Winona responded. She looked at him and was taken aback when he averted his gaze.

"I was wondering if we'll go live with the Shoshones over the summer like we always do?"

It was a peculiar question. Each and every year since Winona's son had been born, they had made it a point to spend two or three months with Winona's people. She insisted on it, in order that Zach might learn their customs and traditions. "Of course we will, Stalking Coyote."

"Do you think Plenty Coups's band will spend time with Spotted Bull's again this year?"

Spotted Bull was Winona's uncle. He had been like a second father to her since the death of his brother at the hands of the Blackfeet. Morning

Dove, his wife, and Willow Woman, his daughter, were two of the best friends Winona had.

The previous Buck Moon and Heat Moon, another band had joined Spotted Bull's on the banks of the Green River. Plenty Coups was their leader. He was as highly respected as her uncle, who had recently become chief after the death of old Broken Paw, and the two had become fast friends.

None of which explained why Winona's son was so interested in whether the two bands would get together again. She slowly lifted the heavy pail, then straightened. The sight of the swirling water under the dripping pail reminded her of an incident that solved the mystery.

It had been during the waning sleeps of the Heat Moon the previous year. The two bands had been about to go their separate ways. Winona and Nate had also been about to say their good-byes and return to their cabin, so she had gone in search of Zach. She had found him on a knoll close to the river, just sitting there with his arms draped over his knees and an odd pained expression on his face. He had jumped up when she'd spoken his name and acted embarrassed that she had caught him there. Why, she hadn't known. Until this very moment.

For it was only now that Winona recalled there had been others at the river that day. Three older girls had been south of the knoll, washing garments. She had not made the connection because her son had never shown any interest in females, but suddenly she understood.

"I expect Plenty Coups will be there," Winona mentioned matter-of-factly. "Perhaps he will invite us to his lodge for a feast as he did the last time."

Zach held his tongue. He didn't want his mother

to suspect that he had grown uncommonly fond of one of the chief's daughters and had been pining for her all during the previous fall and winter. He didn't want *anyone* to know. The overwhelming feeling that had come over him when he had set eyes on her for the first time was unlike any he had ever felt before. It bothered him immensely.

Her mouth quirked, Winona started back up the trail. She would have to tell Nate and counsel with him on how best to handle their son's awakening manhood.

It was a subject they had discussed before, and Winona knew that Nate was not in favor of their son marrying early. He wanted Zach to, as he put it, "see more of the world" before settling down, a notion she regarded as silly. What difference would it make in the long run?

No matter how Nate or she felt, when Zach was ready, he would take a mate, and nothing she or Nate said would dissuade him. Love would run its own course. It always had, it always would.

A pair of ravens abruptly winged low over their heads, the steady beat of their wings bringing Winona out of her reverie. She watched the birds sail westward, in the direction her husband had taken, and hoped he was all right. Wolverines were not to be taken lightly.

She should know, since she had fought one once, many winters ago. It had been during one of Nate's frequent absences, before the children were born, and she had been lucky to survive its onslaught. Years had passed since last she thought of it.

Such encounters happened all too often in the wilderness. So often that whites and Indians alike tended to take them for granted.

In any given month, Winona might spy two or three grizzlies in the vicinity of the lake. Black bears were also regular visitors, as were panthers and wolves. Any one of them would attack her without warning if they were in the mood, but she never fretted over the likelihood. They were simply part and parcel of her everyday life, hazards to be prudently avoided. And when that wasn't possible, she was prepared to defend her life and the lives of her loved ones with her dying breath if need be.

As if on cue, to the north rose a guttural cough. Winona halted and scoured the valley without result.

"That sounded like a griz to me," Zach mentioned as he placed a hand on the smooth butt of his pistol. He wished now that he had brought his rifle. No pistol made was capable of dropping one of the lords of the wild with a single shot, and it was doubtful a charging bear would give him time to reload.

Evelyn squirmed in the cradleboard, prompting Winona to hurry on. Some of the water in the pail sloshed over the rim onto her legs, so she gripped the handle in both hands and held the pail in front of her to steady it.

Presently the cabin appeared. Winona was in such haste to get there that she was mere yards from the door when she realized it hung partway open. She stopped short so unexpectedly that her son nearly blundered into her. Puzzled, she listened but heard no sounds from inside. Yet she was certain she had closed the door behind her when she left, and she whispered as much to Zach.

Holding the pistol in front of him, the youth stepped around his mother. He looked for his father's horse in the corral, but it wasn't there. A knot formed in the pit of his stomach and his mouth went dry. He nervously licked his lips as he stalked to the front wall and ducked so he could peek into the window.

The cabin appeared empty. Zach motioned for his mother to stay put and cat-footed to the doorway. Pushing with his left foot, he swung the door wide open. No shots or shouts rang out. Bending at the waist, he darted inside and confirmed no one was there.

"All clear," Zach reported.

Winona wasted no time in placing the pail on the counter and shrugging out of the cradleboard, which she hung from a stout peg above the bed. "I must have been mistaken," she told her son, even though she was sure that she was not. To be on the safe side, she added, "But we will check around the cabin, just in case."

Zach went to the corner where his Hawken leaned. It was his pride and joy, a gift from his parents. They had bestowed it on him at the last rendezvous, and he had spent at least half an hour every night ever since, cleaning and polishing it until it shone from one end to the other.

Winona grabbed her rifle, an ammo pouch, and a powder horn. She made a point of closing the door behind Zach, then moved to the northeast corner.

In order to prevent anyone from taking them by surprise, Nate had cleared all the brush within a 50-foot radius. Winona saw no one close by or in the trees. She cautiously went on to the next corner.

Zach kept glancing to their rear. Experience had taught him that hostiles could be downright sneaky, and he was not about to lose his hair if he could help it.

Suddenly Winona stopped. In the dirt at the base of the north wall were a number of moccasin tracks. She pointed them out to Zach, who nodded. Sinking onto her left knee, she scrutinized them. By their shape it was plain that they had not been made by Shoshones.

A very worried Zach kept his eyes on the trees. If there were enemies about, he reflected, that was where they would be. A slight creak above them prompted him to glance up at the roof, and he learned he had been wrong. The forest wasn't the only place the hostiles might be hiding.

Over the edge of the roof plummeted four buckskin clad warriors.

Chapter Three

Nate King was worried sick by the time he paused on a grassy bench overlooking the verdant valley he had staked out as his own. The lake sparkled like a shimmering jewel in the brilliant sunshine, and to the southeast several elk were visible on a low slope. He couldn't see the cabin.

The nine warriors had descended the bench in single file and stayed in single file once they reached the valley floor. It was a tactic typically employed when a war party knew it was nearing an enemy camp.

Nate threw off all caution. His family was in mortal peril, and for all he knew they might have already been attacked. He pushed the big black stallion at a breakneck pace, vaulting logs and plowing through thickets rather than going around them.

The woods were so thick that Nate didn't catch a glimpse of the cabin until he was within a hundred yards of it. His innate caution made him slow down even though an inner voice screamed at him to rush on in there before it was too late.

In a stand of spruce, Nate drew rein and dismounted. Ground-hitching the stallion, he padded forward and cocked the Hawken. In the brush at the edge of the clearing, he squatted and parted the branches in front of him.

All appeared tranquil. The cabin was quiet and there was no sign of hostile warriors.

Nate glided to the east, to a vantage point behind an old stump situated 40 feet from the front door. It was closed. The glare on the windows prevented him from seeing inside, but he thought he detected movement. He was about to stride into the open when the latch rasped and the door opened.

Out walked a warrior painted for war.

Instantly Nate brought the Hawken up and sighted on the center of the man's chest. In his mind's eye he saw his slaughtered family lying in bloody pools on the cabin floor. His finger started to close on the trigger.

Then the warrior looked right at Nate and smiled. Holding his right hand in front of his neck with the palm outward and the index and second fingers extended skyward, the warrior raised his hand until the extended fingers were as high as the top of his head.

It was sign language. The gesture meant 'friend.'

Nate blinked, and slowly lowered the rifle as recognition set in. The style of the warrior's buckskins and the pair of long braids on either side of his head were the earmarks of a Crow. The tribe was generally friendly to whites, although there had been isolated instances where the two sides had clashed.

Looking closer, Nate was startled to find that he knew this particular warrior. Lowering the Hawken, he stepped from concealment.

The Crow's hands flew in more sign language, saying, in effect, "My heart is glad that we meet again, Grizzly Killer. It has been too many moons since last we shared a pipe."

Nate glanced at the doorway. Other warriors were inside, staring at him.

"You do remember me?" the warrior went on. "I am Two Humps. You saved my son from the renegade white who was known as the Invincible One."

Nate remembered all too well. A man by the name of Jacob Pierce had tricked the Crows into believing he could not be killed and had instigated a bloodbath that resulted in the loss of many innocent lives. During the conflict, Two Humps had befriended Nate and Nate's mentor, Shakespeare McNair. They had parted on the best of terms.

Warily, Nate set the stock of the Hawken on the ground and leaned the rifle against his leg to free his hands. "I remember you," he signed. "I remember telling you where to find my lodge, but I did not think I would see you again so soon." Nate gazed over the warrior's shoulder. "I see you have others with you. I hope they did not harm my family."

"What kind of man would I be if I repaid your kindness with treachery?" Two Humps beckoned. "Come see for yourself. Your wife and son and daughter are fine."

At that juncture the warriors inside parted, and out came Winona with Evelyn in her arms. Zach followed. Mother and son hurried over, the youth armed with his pistol and knife.

Nate finally allowed himself to relax. If the

Crows were up to no good, they would hardly have let the boy keep any weapons. He embraced each in turn. "For a while there I was mighty worried," he admitted softly so only they could hear.

"That makes two of us, husband," Winona said, giving the Crows an indignant look. She had feared for their lives when the four warriors jumped from the roof. One had torn the rifle from her grasp as three more rushed around the corner of the cabin and bore her to the earth. Only instead of slashing her throat, they had stripped her of her knife and pinned her until she quieted. The same had been done to Zach. When both of them were safely unarmed, Two Humps had appeared and explained the purpose for his visit in sign. He had apologized for their rough treatment and given back their weapons. All this Winona now told her husband, adding, "He claimed that he was afraid we might shoot him before he had a chance to explain himself, so that is why he took us by surprise."

Nate pursed his lips. The precaution made sense. It didn't do for strangers to waltz up to a camp or a cabin unannounced. Some mountaineers would shoot first and ask questions later. "I reckon we can't hold it against him," he said.

"I can," Zach groused. "I've got a goose egg on the back of my noggin. They were awful rough on me."

"You're almost an adult now, son," Nate reminded him. "So they treated you like one."

The suggestion that he was so close to manhood made Zach beam. "That's right, I am. I suppose I shouldn't hold a grudge. I might have done the same if I was in their moccasins."

Two Humps advanced. "I trust there are no bad

feelings," he signed earnestly. "Please accept my apology."

There was no denying the warrior's sincerity. Nate put his hand on the Crow's shoulder before signing, "You did what you had to do. Let us go inside. We will smoke a pipe together and you can tell me what has brought you so far from your country."

The warriors in the cabin respectfully backed out of the way and ringed themselves around the room. Most were younger than Two Humps. A notable exception was a man who appeared years older and wore a sorrowful countenance at all times. The younger ones were amazed by the wooden lodge and never tired of running their fingers over every odd object they came across. One even stuck his head into the fireplace and wound up with soot on his forehead and cheeks.

While this was going on, Nate and Two Humps sat at the table and shared a pipe. The Crow smacked the chair a few times before he would sit down and gave it a hard shake to verify it was strong enough to hold his weight.

With the amenities disposed of, Nate regarded the warrior intently. The younger warriors stopped their shenanigans to pay close attention, while the older man walked over to the table, his features as somber as a storm cloud.

"This is my brother, Bull Standing With Cow," Two Humps introduced them. "His heart is heavy because he has lost his woman and his son." The warrior motioned at the others. "All our hearts our heavy. Twenty sleeps ago our village was raided by a large band of Lakota. They struck early in the morning when the sun had not yet cleared the horizon. Many of our people were slain, and many horses were stolen."

Bull Standing With Cow grunted. "They also took three of our women," he signed. "One is my daughter, Fetches Water. She has only seen fourteen winters."

Nate sympathized. He'd be devastated if the same thing ever happened to his wife or children. It was a long harbored dread of his that one day he would come back from a trapping trip and find them gone, kidnapped by one of his many enemies.

"These Lakota have raided us before," Two Humps went on. "They are Oglalas."

"I have heard of them," Nate signed. They lived in the region of the South Platte river and had a reputation for being an extremely warlike tribe. The Lakota were more often called the 'Sioux' by most whites, the name stemming from an old French word for them, 'Nadowessioux.'

"They know no mercy, these Oglalas," Two Humps said. "They killed all they could and then escaped before we could gather our scattered horses. Many brave men died that day protecting those they loved."

Nate did not need to be reminded how bloody Indian warfare could be. He had witnessed it first-hand. "So now you are on your way to Oglala country to try and rescue the women?" he speculated.

"Yes," Two Humps confirmed. "Bull Standing With Cow is sick inside with fear for his daughter. He wanted to come by himself, but I would not let him."

A young warrior whose stocky body rippled with muscles motioned in contempt and signed sharply, "The Lakota do not scare us! We will make them regret what they have done! They will learn that the Absaroka are not timid rabbits they can attack at will!"

Two Humps frowned. "That is He Dog. He has never fought the Lakota. He was off hunting when our village was raided, or he would not be so eager to confront them again."

The stocky warrior was offended. "I fear no one!" he signed emphatically. "Let any man who claims I do tell me so to my face."

Bull Standing With Cow glowered at the younger man. "No one here questions your bravery. But courage alone does not win battles. A man must have wisdom. He must be able to think clearly at all times if he is to prevail."

"Are you saying I do not?"

"I am saying you have much to learn before you will be a warrior the equal of Two Humps. Now be still and let your elders speak. Or have you lost your manners as well as your judgment?" Bull Standing With Cow shot back.

Tension hung thick in the air. Nate knew that his friend had his work cut out for him. The Crows would have a hard enough time without petty bickering among themselves. "Just the nine of you against the whole Oglala tribe," he commented. "Those are not good odds."

"Nine were all that could be spared," Two Humps responded. "The rest had to stay to safeguard our village." His dark eyes locked on Nate. "I was hoping we could lower the odds, Grizzly Killer. We have all seen for ourselves that your medicine is very powerful. You were the one who defeated the Iron Warrior. So I have come to you for help."

Winona was in the act of making a pot of coffee. She had carried the pot to the fireplace and was about to start a small fire when she happened to glance around and saw the Crow warrior sign his last statement. Forgetting the fire for the time being, she walked to the table and stood at her husband's elbow to await his response.

Nate did not quite know what to say. He liked Two Humps and considered the man a friend, but they were not all that close. The truth was that they hardly knew one another. In his opinion it was downright presumptuous of the Crow to ask him to risk his life. He was all set to decline, but the image of a terrified 14-year-old gave him pause.

Two Humps seemed to read his thoughts. "I know I ask a lot of you, Grizzly Killer. But there is no one else to whom we can turn." He leaned forward. "We do not know the country of the Lakotas very well. You do. Or at least you told me once that you had crossed the great sea of grass when you came to these mountains to live, and another time when you visited the Mandans."

Bull Standing With Cow broke in. "We do not want you to do our fighting for us, Grizzly Killer. We only ask that you guide us to the land of Oglalas by the shortest possible route. Once you have done that, you can turn around and head home if you want." His weathered features shifted. A haunted aspect came over them. "Please, Grizzly Killer. As one father to another, I plead with you to help me rescue my daughter. I do not want her to spend the rest of her life as the unwilling wife of a Lakota who treats her worse than he does his dog." He clasped his hands together. "Please."

Winona could tell that the heartfelt appeal touched her husband deeply. Knowing him as well as she did herself, she spoke up in English before he could reply. "Think this over carefully, husband. The Sioux are formidable foes. If they learn that you helped the Crows, they will not rest until they have taken their revenge."

"A man can't turn his back on another in need," Nate noted. "My mother used to quote from the Good Book a lot. And one of the sayings always stuck in my head. 'Do unto others as you would have them do unto you.'"

"White ways are not our ways," Winona countered. "The Sioux have never heard of your Good Book. All they care about is counting coup on every white they find in their land."

Nate shifted to face her. "The girl is the main issue. How can we turn our backs on her?"

"We do not know her."

"Does that mean we just leave her to her fate? If she were ours, we wouldn't rest until she was safe and sound."

"She is *not* ours," Winona stressed. It wasn't that she had anything against the Crow girl. It was the fact that there was a definite possibility she would never set eyes on her husband again if he ventured into Lakota country that made her balk at the proposal.

"I don't see where that makes a difference. If Zach were missing and I went to Two Humps for help, you know as well as I do that he'd do all he could on our behalf."

Winona knew a losing cause when she saw one. Sighing, she tenderly touched his chin and said, "Sometimes you are too good for your own good. Very well. We will go with them."

"We?"

"Stalking Coyote is old enough to go on a raid. And I will not be left behind."

Young Zachary King had been lounging against the counter with his arms folded across his chest. He did not have much interest in the proceedings since he knew his father would go the moment the Crow asked and assumed that he'd be left behind once again to watch over his mother and sister. It was the same old story every time his father went traipsing off. So he was all the more shocked when he heard his mother say he should be in on the raid. Excitement quickened his pulse as he straightened and nodded. "I think Ma's right," he declared. "Some of the Shoshone boys my age have gone on raids already. And you said just a while ago, Pa, that I'm almost a full-growed man."

Nate wanted to bite his tongue. He had made the comment to bolster his son's esteem, not to imply the boy was mature enough to go on the war path. Having nothing better to retort, he responded curtly, "You stay out of this, young 'un. You're not a man yet, and until you are, what I say goes."

"What we *both* say goes," Winona corrected him, "and I say our son should join you. He will learn much. And his rifle will come in handy if the Lakotas spot us."

"There you go with that 'us' business again," Nate griped. "A raid is no place for a woman with a baby."

"Evelyn will pose no problem. I will tend to her at all times," Winona pledged. "And you know that she will not cry and give us away while we are on the trail, so you need not worry in that regard."

Nate gazed fondly at their infant. He had never quite grown accustomed to the Shoshone custom of toting a baby out into the woods every time it bawled and hanging the cradleboard from a high limb until it quieted down, but he had to admit the tactic worked. Four or five times of such harsh treatment was enough to stop most babies from ever blubbering aloud. They learned early on to keep their emotions under control, or else.

It was a hard but essential lesson. The wail of an infant might give a village away to marauding enemies. Older children, when they played, knew to keep their voices down. It was a price they had to pay in the name of survival.

Two Humps had been watching the trapper and his wife with growing anxiety. When they fell silent, he signed, "Is your woman against your going, Grizzly Killer?"

"She does not want anything to happen to me," Nate hedged. "She thinks it best that I take my whole family along, and I agree."

Zach whooped for joy and spun in a circle.

Winona smiled and squeezed her husband's shoulder in gratitude.

He Dog sputtered and stormed toward the table. "Do my ears hear right?" he angrily signed. "This white man wants to bring a *woman* on a raid? I will not hear of it."

Two Humps turned on the younger warrior and half rose out of his chair. For the benefit of the Kings, he used sign language instead of the Crow tongue. "It is not your place to say who comes and who does not. As for a woman making war, need I remind you that there is a woman warrior living with Long Hair's band who has counted more coup than you have? If Grizzly Killer wants his wife to come, she can."

"She will slow us down," He Dog signed. "And these mixed-breed cubs of hers have—"

Nate King exploded out of his chair. He reached the stocky warrior in two bounds and slammed his fist into the Crow's chin. He Dog was knocked back against the wall. Belatedly the hothead clawed for a knife on his right hip. Nate did not let him draw it. Another right to the jaw rocked

He Dog to one side. A left jab and an uppercut stiffened him as rigid as a board. And a round-house right flattened the man in his tracks.

Breathing heavily from his exertion, Nate slowly drew one of his pistols and pivoted. Some of the other warriors had started to move toward him but they stopped at sight of the flintlock.

"Enough!" Two Humps urgently signed. "We came here to ask Grizzly Killer's help, not to insult his woman or to attack him."

All the Crows but one heeded their leader. A lanky warrior made as if to lift his lance but checked his movement when two loud clicks sounded.

Winona King had her rifle in hand. Zach had produced his pistol. Both guns were trained on the lanky warrior's torso. He had only to see the fires blazing in the Shoshone woman's eyes to change his mind about aiding his friend.

Moving to his family, Nate placed his pistol on the counter within ready reach and signed, "You all heard He Dog. He had no right to heap abuse on us. He had no right to say those things about my wife."

The Crows exchanged glances. Little hostility was evident.

Winona believed that most of the warriors agreed with her husband. But since it was her ability which had been called into question, she elected to demonstrate to them that she would be useful in the days ahead. "I want all of you to step outside," she signed, and exited without bothering to confirm that they complied with her request.

Stepping to the left, Winona searched the woods and spotted a large knot on a tree about as far from the cabin as an arrow could fly.

Voices murmured. The Crows were gathered in

a group, a few eyeing her skeptically. Nate and Zach were by the window.

"See that knot?" Winona asked. Without waiting for a response, she aimed, compensating for the distance by hiking the barrel a hair, held her breath as her husband had taught her to do, counted to three in her head, and lightly stroked the trigger. Smoke and lead belched from the barrel, the smoke forming a cloud which momentarily hid the tree from view. She lowered the gun and signed, "I would be grateful if one of you would go examine the tree."

Two warriors bounded off. They hollered on reaching the trunk and pointed excitedly at the knot.

Two Humps nodded and smiled. "They say you hit the knot in the center," he signed. "I am impressed. It is a feat that would challenge our best bowmen."

"So there is no one else who would speak against me?" Winona asked, deliberately staring at the lanky warrior.

No one did.

Nate walked over to Winona and looped an arm around her shoulders. He was so proud of her, he was fit to bust. For the umpteenth time since the day they became man and wife, amazement came over him that so lovely and competent a woman had chosen him to be her mate. For the life of him he did not know what he had done to deserve her.

"We will go off by ourselves and hold a council," Two Humps said. "I will ask each man to give his opinion, and those who still do not want a woman along will be told to return to our village."

He Dog had to be carted from the cabin like a sack of grain. He was still unconscious and blood dribbled from the corner of his mouth.

The Crows melted into the forest to the south. Zach waited until they were out of sight, then laughed and exclaimed, "Tarnation! You sure showed them, Ma! And Pa! You tore into that man like a riled grizzly!"

"It's no laughing matter," Nate scolded. "I shouldn't have lost my temper. He Dog doesn't strike me as the forgiving type. I'll have to keep my eyes skinned the whole time from now on."

"I'll watch him like a hawk too," Zach volunteered. "If he tries to make trouble, we'll teach him some manners."

Nate hoped it wouldn't come to that, but he had to face facts. They hadn't even left yet and already he had earned the hatred of one Crow and the ill will of a second. If he had a lick of common sense, he would back out before it was too late. But he couldn't. Not with the welfare of the 14-year-old girl at stake.

"Let us go inside," Winona said. "I must check on our daughter and begin to pack." She held her rifle at arm's length. "I must remember to bring extra ammunition. Something tells me that we are going to need it."

Chapter Four

At first light the next morning the war party of vengeful Crows and the King family departed. Not one of the Crows backed out, not even He Dog or his lanky friend, Runs Against.

Nate wasn't surprised. He Dog had a score to settle. The dour looks the pair frequently bestowed on him when they thought he wouldn't notice were ample proof they had it in for him.

The other Crows, though, were as nice as could be. Bull Standing With Cow, especially, pledged his undying friendship, and told Nate in sign language that for as long as they both lived, his lodge was Nate's lodge and anything he owned was Nate's for the taking.

Since Nate had been asked to serve as their guide, he led the way to a notch in the ring of heavily forested mountains to the east. Beyond it, they paused on a wide shelf to enjoy a sweeping panoramic vista of the many stark lower peaks and rolling green foothills below, as well as the well-nigh limitless expanse of prairie stretching eastward for as far as the eye could see. It was a breathtaking sight.

A switchback brought them to a meadow luxuriant with grass and flowers. Presently they came on a gurgling stream and paralleled its winding course lower to where it flowed into a swift but shallow river. This was the Big Thompson, as a few of the mountaineer men called it, and further on the river coursed through the spectacular Big Thompson canyon where towering rock ramparts hemmed the party in on both sides.

Some of the warriors muttered uneasily and cast distrustful glances at the remote heights. Nate didn't blame them. He had never much liked the closed-in sort of feeling that riding through the canyon always sparked. And, too, there was the ever present danger of massive boulders falling from on high. Twice in the past he had narrowly escaped being crushed to a pulp when that happened.

Which explained why Nate so seldom took the Big Thompson route. There was another way into this remote valley, a winding trail long used by Indians and animals alike. The going was much easier and more open. Unfortunately, it would have brought them out of the mountains a good 20 miles south of where the Big Thompson canyon would.

Winona rode behind her husband, their daughter nestled in the cradleboard on her back. Her mount was a favorite surefooted mare. In addition to her rifle, she had a knife and a pistol.

The Shoshone woman did not fail to note the bitter looks that He Dog and Runs Against gave her man. She didn't let on how pleased she was to see He Dog's swollen, puffy lips and cheeks. Whenever the party stopped to rest, she made it a point to keep her eyes on the two. If either lifted a finger against her husband, she would shoot them dead without hesitation.

Zach was also watching his father's back. When he thought of it. He was so thrilled at being allowed to go on the raid that his blood practically sang in his veins. He was giddy at the prospect of counting coup.

Shoshones measured manhood by the same standard as the Sioux, the Cheyenne, the Crows and Blackfeet and many other tribes; by brave deeds performed in the heat of battle. When Zach visited with his mother's people every summer, he heard countless tales of the exploits of famous warriors. War was all the boys his age liked to talk about.

In order to rise in public esteem, a Shoshone boy had to count coup on his enemies. The more coup he counted, the more esteemed he became. It was as simple as that.

Young Zach was no stranger to bloodshed. He had a number of coups to his credit already. He had even killed. But he wanted more coups, the more the better, and he prayed that the Great Mystery would grant him his heart's desire when they struck Lakota country.

In the meantime, the boy was intoxicated with excitement. He felt more alive than he ever had. The very air seemed invigorating, and his whole body tingled at times. He could barely sit still in the saddle and constantly shifted to take in all there was to see.

So it was that Zach was the first to notice movement at the rim of the towering cliff to their right just as the war party entered a shadowed stretch where the walls narrowed, affording them barely enough room for their horses to proceed in single file.

Zach looked closer. Eagles sometimes perched on the rim and he liked to watch them take flight. Occasionally, bighorn sheep appeared, prancing about the sheer cliffs as if they were on solid ground. But the thing he saw moving was huge and brown, and for a few moments he imagined it was a grizzly tumbling end over end. Then he recognized it for what it was. "Pa! One of the boulders is falling!"

Nate took one glance and hollered, "Ride! Ride!" while motioning for the Crows to do just that. He jabbed his heels into the stallion's flanks and took off at a gallop, hugging the wall to his right to avoid a misstep which might send him sliding into the river.

The pounding clatter of heavy hooves drummed in Nate's ears. He would much rather have moved aside so his wife and son could go past him, but there wasn't enough room. Above him erupted a tremendous booming crash as the cabin-sized boulder bounced off a spur of rock.

A look back showed the warriors were in full flight.

The boulder was falling faster, gaining momentum rapidly. It smashed against the cliff time and again. Deafening crashes resembled the peal of thunder.

The trail grew steeper, forcing Nate to concentrate on his riding to the exclusion of all else. A short slope brought him to a wide level area where he could give the stallion its head, but instead he cut to the right and slowed so Winona and Zach could get in front of him as he wanted. Once they were past, he fell into place beside Two Humps.

The last warrior in line was also the youngest. His name was Feather Earring and he made no attempt to conceal his rising fright. Nate saw him look upward again and again, gauging whether he would get out of the way in time.

It was close. Feather Earring was almost to the bottom of the short slope when the boulder impacted in the middle of the trail less than ten feet behind him. The ground shook as if from an earthquake and the high walls themselves seemed to shake and shimmy. A thick cloud of dust swirled skyward above the boulder as dirt and small stones and other debris rained down.

Nate smiled in relief. They were safe. Or so he believed until the clouds parted and the circular boulder rolled down the slope in their wake, going faster and faster with every foot it traveled.

"Go! Go!" Nate cried, urging the Crows on. Not that they needed to be prompted. They all saw the immense monster hard on their heels and lashed their mounts with their quirts or their reins.

Feathered Earring let out a yelp. His horse had stumbled and nearly fallen and he had lost precious ground to the stone titan. He had a bow in hand which he frantically applied to his mount.

Ahead lay a bend. If they reached it, they would be safe. But *could* they? Nate wondered as he flew across the level area with the wind in his hair and dust in his nostrils. The rumbling crunch of the boulder was growing louder by the second. He could have sworn it was right behind him.

Incongruously, little Evelyn was smiling and giggling, having great fun. Her cherubic face and tiny fingers poked from the top of the cradleboard. When the mare swept around the bend and nearly lost its footing, she squealed in delight.

Zach was so close to his mother that he had to

haul on the reins of his pinto in order not to crash into the tottering mare. The trail broadened, enabling him to veer to the right. He went a score of yards, then drew rein to see if the Crows gained cover. Two Humps, Bull Standing With Cow, and He Dog came around the bend one right after the other. So did two other warriors. To his dismay, there was no sign of his father.

Nate had slowed again to goad the warriors on. Runs Against flashed past him. So did Flying Hawk and Long Forelock. Feather Earring was yards back, flailing his flagging horse with all his strength. It was doing no good.

The boulder was almost upon them. Rolling at an incredible rate of speed, with part of it in the river and part on dry land, it was like a raging bull or a runaway steam engine. There was no stopping it. Gravel, branches and brush were smashed to bits under its incalculable weight.

Nate could delay no longer. Slapping his legs, he sped around the bend, twisting as he did. He saw the nose of the young warrior's mount appear. And then there was a horrid screech and he saw Feather Earring and the animal caught under the onrushing goliath. There was wild desperation in the Crow's eyes as the boulder rolled up over him. Man and horse were bent and flattened and reduced to a commingled reddish mass of oozing gore, pulverized flesh, and shattered bones.

The boulder plowed across the river, throwing a wide spray in its wake. It rammed into the opposite wall with an ear-blistering concussion, fracturing the craggy surface in a regular spider's web of small cracks and wider clefts.

Panic seized some of the Crows's horses. The animals pitched and plunged, whinnying in a frenzy of unbridled fear. The warriors held on for dear life. Flying Hawk was thrown onto his shoulder and lay there, dazed. He Dog was nearly unhorsed but grabbed his sorrel's mane and belabored it about the head and neck with his fists until it calmed down and stood trembling like a frightened child.

The black stallion quaked a few times but that was all. Nate rode over to Winona and Zach and placed a hand on each of them in turn. He did not say anything. Words weren't necessary.

The Crows called a halt then and there. A council was held. Since they conversed in their tongue, the Kings had no idea what was being discussed until afterward when Two Humps summarized the dispute.

Four of the warriors had been in favor of going back. Led by Long Forelock, the faction maintained that the death of Feather Earring was bad medicine, an omen of worse to come.

Bull Standing With Cow made an eloquent appeal, asking those who had children if they would be so eager to give up if it was their child and not his. He also pointed out to those who were not married that they had a sacred obligation to do all in their power to help members of their tribe whenever and wherever help was needed.

The four men changed their minds.

The Crows wanted to do right by Feather Earring but there were no trees nearby, nor was there enough left of him to scrape up and bury. They compromised. From a gravel bed in the river they gathered enough to cover the pulped remains with an inch-thick layer. A simple ceremony was performed and the journey resumed.

From there on until the end of the canyon, each and every one of them rode with his or her eyes glued to the boulder-strewn heights. They avoided

53

David Thompson

making any undue loud noises.

At last the canyon widened and rolling foothills unfolded before them.

The sun hung high in the afternoon sky, but not high enough to justify stopping for the night. Nate pushed on, wending lower past earthen and sandstone cliffs.

They were shy of the prairie by just a few miles when twilight overtook them. Nate knew the region as well as he did the proverbial back of his hand. He selected a spacious clearing near the river for their camp. Enclosed by cottonwoods and willows, it offered adequate shelter from the wind and screened their fire from prying eyes.

The Crows were in a somber mood. Saddened by the loss of their companion, they were not much interested in eating or talking.

Nate made coffee and a stew from a rabbit he shot. He did the butchering while his wife went off by the river to feed their daughter.

Winona did not care to have the Crows watch her breast-feed. Shoshones as a rule were not shy about normal bodily functions, but she had learned that other people did not share the Shoshone outlook. Some whites, for instance, considered it a sin for a woman to expose her breasts in public. Some Indians, the Cheyennes foremost among them, were just as reserved about nudity. She did not know the Crow attitude, but she was taking no chances. In the interests of harmony, she sat at the water's edge with her back to the men and cradled Evelyn in her arms.

The child sucked greedily, kneading Winona's supple flesh with her small fingers. Nate had once told Winona that among his people it was not uncommon for a mother to stop breast-feeding when an infant was no older than a year and a half. The revelation had shocked her.

Among the Shoshones, a mother often breast-fed until the child was three or even four years of age. Her people were of the conviction that doing so instilled an even temperament. Cutting a child off early crimped the child's character, contributing to insolence and rebellion later in life.

Soon Evelyn had drunk her fill and was dozing in perfect bliss. Winona covered herself and gently rocked her daughter, staring down into that innocent face, her heart brimming with love.

Winona was glad that their second child had turned out to be a girl. Boys were fine—she loved Zach as dearly as she did Evelyn—but it was nice to have a girl she could rear as her mother had reared her. She looked forward to passing on the many lessons she had learned at Morning Dew's knee.

Over at the string of tethered horses, Zach King was grooming his pinto. It was a nightly ritual of his ever since his father traded for the animal.

The terrible incident in the canyon had dampened Zach's enthusiasm. Try as he might, he couldn't get the awful image of the young warrior going down under that boulder from his mind. But for the grace of the good Lord, that might have been him, or his mother, or his father. It impressed him as nothing else could that the raid should not be treated as a lark. It was a serious, grave affair which might result in the deaths of all of them if they weren't almighty careful.

Suddenly Zach became aware that he was no longer alone. Turning, he was startled to find He Dog a few yards off, regarding him with open disdain. He ignored the hothead and went back to stroking the pinto with a horsehair brush.

David Thompson

Footsteps came closer. The Crow uttered a mocking laugh.

Zach slowly turned again. The warrior was so close that he could smell the bear fat in He Dog's hair. Making his face as blank as a slate, he set the brush on the pinto's back and signed, "Question. You want?"

He Dog shouldered Zach aside to stand next to the mount. "You call this a horse, white dog?" he signed haughtily. "I would not give it to a girl to ride."

Anger flared in Zach and he clenched his fists. He was all set to take a swing when it occurred to him that might be exactly what the warrior wanted him to do. He Dog was goading him into a fight, probably counting on his father to rush over and get involved.

Plastering a fake smile on his face, Zach said in English, "Why, you mangy polecat. You're plumb no account any way I lay my sights. If you had any brains, you'd know that getting my pa riled is as dumb as can be." Switching to Shoshone, he added, "Your heart is as foul as buffalo droppings. If I were a warrior, I would kill you and be done with you."

He Dog glared. He did not need to understand either language to know that he had been insulted. He raised an arm as if to backhand the boy, then looked up, frowned, and walked off without another gesture.

Bull Standing With Cow strolled up. His kindly eyes conveyed regret, and something more. "I saw, Stalking Coyote," he signed. "If I did not need his help so much, I would tell him to leave. Please bear with him until my daughter is safe."

"I will try," Zach promised.

An awkward few moments went by. Bull Standing With Cow sighed and patted the mare. "My daughter is not much older than you," he signed. "She was just taking an interest in boys. In another winter she would have married, and in two or three I would have grandchildren to sit on my knee."

"It can still happen. We will save her. Watch and see."

The Crow father gazed into the darkness. "I wish I had your confidence, Stalking Coyote. But I have lived too long. I know that good intentions do not always insure events will turn out as we would like them to. Sometimes matters are taken out of our hands."

"We will do all we can to help you. You know that."

"Yes," Bull Standing With Cow signed. "Your father is an honorable man. The Shoshones think highly of him. The Utes, too, I hear. As do my people. He is like the Blanket Chief, straight and true in all he does."

The Blanket Chief, Zach knew, was a mountain man named Jim Bridger, perhaps the single most widely respected white man living west of the Mississippi. The warrior had given his father quite a compliment.

Over by the fire, Nate King rose. He saw his son signing to Bull Standing With Cow but could not make out what was being said. Picking up his Hawken, he strolled to the river.

The night was moonless. A pall of gloom hung over the camp, befitting the mood of the Crows.

Nate spied the silhouette of his wife against the lighter backdrop of the river. Her gaze was on the myriad of stars sparkling like jewels in the inky firmament. "Are you fixing to spend the whole night in this spot?" he joked.

Winona grinned. "It is so peaceful here, husband. Our daughter is sound asleep and I do not want to disturb her yet."

Sinking down and crossing his legs in front of him, Nate listened to the whisper of the current and the sigh of the wind in the cottonwoods. "I see what you mean," he commented softly. The tension drained out of him like water from a sieve and he leaned back on his hands. "I hope to high heaven we haven't bitten off more than we can chew," he voiced his uppermost concern.

"Are you worried?"

"I'd be speaking with two tongues if I claimed otherwise. But we've gone up against worse. I reckon we can handle whatever comes along."

Of the many traits her husband possessed that Winona King admired, his perseverance in the face of adversity was foremost. When up against an insurmountable obstacle, he liked to say, "Where there's a will, there's a way." And then he would go on to overcome it.

Winona tenderly placed her hand on his wrist and leaned over to peck him on the jaw. "I am sure you are right," she whispered.

Nate kissed her lightly on the lips. Two of her fingers traced the outline of his knuckles and he could feel the smooth flesh at the tips where formerly her nails had been.

Years ago, shortly after they met, Winona's parents had been slain by Blackfeet. In keeping with Shoshone custom, as a token of her grief, she had chopped the ends off of a couple of fingers on her left hand. There had been a time when the mere thought of her sacrifice would have caused Nate to break out in goosebumps. But no longer. He had grown to accept the custom, just as he had grown to accept a great many things he once had branded as plain obscene.

Life was warped in that regard. Back in the States there were plenty of whites who hated Indians simply because they were different. Savages, the whites called them. Yet if those who did the name calling could spend some time with those they hated so much, they'd learn, just as Nate had, that when all was said and done, the red man and the white man were closer kin than most would admit.

"I think tomorrow Zach and I will take turns riding behind everyone else," Winona mentioned.

"So you can keep better tabs on He Dog and his pard," Nate guessed.

"It is not wise to have an enemy riding at your back. You never know when you might sprout more arrows than a porcupine has quills."

Nate chuckled. "Goodness gracious, dearest. You're starting to sound a lot like Shakespeare McNair."

"I wish he were with us now."

"So do I." Nate missed his closest friend and mentor greatly. A few moons back Shakespeare and his Flathead wife, Blue Water Woman, had gone on a long delayed visit to her people. Shakespeare had told him it would be unlikely they'd be back at their cabin, located about 25 miles north of the King homestead, until the first leaves started to fall.

Evelyn stirred, and Winona reached down to cover the infant's face. As she straightened, she peered through the trees toward the prairie and tensed. "Husband, look."

Far out on the plain, barely visible, flickered a dancing point of light.

"Another camp fire," Nate realized. He almost jumped up and dashed to their own fire to put it out. But it was small and shielded by the vegetation. He doubted whoever was out there had spotted the pale glow. "I'd best have a talk with Two Humps. The Crows have to help take turns keeping watch tonight, whether they like the notion or not."

Winona took his hand as he rose. "No matter what happens on our journey, I want you to know you have done the right thing. You make me proud to be your woman."

"Thanks," Nate said. He didn't add that if anything happened to their children or her, knowing he had done right would be damn small consolation. Yet he was thinking it.

Chapter Five

The spot was easy to find, thanks to the acrid scent of smoke lingering in the brisk morning air and the spiraling white tendrils that wafted upward now and again from the smoldering embers of the camp fire.

Nate crouched in high grass a score of feet away and scanned the vicinity. Even at that distance he knew white men had been responsible. The charred remains formed a wide circle, indicating the fire had been a big one. And only white men made fires so large that they dared not get too close for fear of being singed. Indians invariably built small ones so they could sit close to the flames to keep warm.

Rising, Nate cautiously emerged from cover. It puzzled him that the camp had been made right out in the open in a small flattened area rather than in a gully or near a knoll where there would have been protection from the stiff night winds and hostile eyes would have been less apt to spot the blaze. No mountain man worthy of the name would have camped there. It had to have been greenhorns, Nate reasoned.

The trapper found tracks, but they only added to his puzzlement. There was one set, and one set alone. Boot prints, judging by the size and shape. And the man had been afoot. There was not a single hoof track anywhere.

Nate hunkered and scratched his chin, pondering. The boots confirmed his hunch about a greenhorn being to blame. Experienced mountaineers preferred lightweight moccasins to unwieldy store bought footwear.

It bothered Nate that the man was afoot. Being stranded without a horse was a certain death warrant for any man not able to fend for himself. The wilderness was a harsh taskmaster. Those not able to wrestle with the wild on its own terms inevitably paid for their weakness with their lives.

The tracks bore eastward. Evidently the man was on his way back to civilization. But for him to expect to cross the vast prairie on foot was akin to expecting a miracle. Grizzlies and other predators were more numerous than fleas on an old coonhound. And hostiles were everywhere.

Rising, Nate held his Hawken aloft and waved it from side to side, the signal they had agreed on if it was safe for the rest to join him. They were hidden in a wash over a hundred yards off and promptly appeared, riding abreast, with Zach leading the black stallion.

"What did you find?" Winona asked as she drew rein.

Nate explained in sign language, pointing out the tracks as he did. Then he surprised the Crows by signing, "I would like to speak to this white man. He left a short while ago, so it should not take long for us to catch up with him."

He Dog promptly objected. "What do we care about this stupid white man? Bull Standing With Cow's daughter is more important. I say we press on. This will only delay us."

Nate faced the father. "He Dog has a point. The decision should be yours. If you want, the rest of you can ride to the northeast and I will overtake you before the sun is straight overhead."

The Crow reflected a few moments. "A short delay will not matter much. And I do not want us to be separated. We will all go after this white man."

"Thank you," Nate said sincerely. Forking leather, he galloped on the greenhorn's trail. The man had not made good time. Within ten minutes Nate spied a solitary figure plodding along under the brilliant sun.

"I should go on ahead," Nate signed. "He might shoot if he mistakes us for enemies."

"Can I tag along, Pa?" Zach asked. He was burning with curiosity to learn more about the stranger. Other than the annual rendezvous and regular visits by his Uncle Shakespeare, encounters with white men were few and far between.

"No," Nate replied, deliberately looking at He Dog. "You'd best stay here with your ma." He rode off before the hothead or Runs Against could complain, holding to a trot until he was close enough for the greenhorn to hear him.

Since Nate was not partial to being shot at, he hollered in greeting, "Hold up there, friend! I'd like a few words with you!"

The man slowly stopped and turned. His movements were awkward and sluggish, as if he were drunk. His eyes narrowed and he peered uncertainly around him as if he could not see well.

Nate moved closer. He was shocked to discover the man was unarmed. No rifle, no pistol, no knife, nothing. Other than a worn set of grungy woolen clothes and a leather possibles bag, the man had no possessions whatsoever. "I mean you no harm. I'm a white man, like you."

The greenhorn's thin lips quirked upward. "White?" he croaked.

Nate came to a halt. He'd come across men on the verge of starvation before and recognized the signs. The sluggishness and confusion were typical. Plus the man was skin and bones, the clothes hanging limp on his wasted frame. "My handle is Nate King. I'm a free trapper. Who might you be, hoss?"

"Emmet Carter," the man rasped. His eyes commenced to water, but whether from the sunlight or because he was crying, Nate couldn't tell.

"Well, Emmet, it appears to me that you could use some help. What in blazes are you doing out here in the middle of nowhere all by your lonesome?"

Carter licked his lips and coughed. "I'm heading home, to Maryland."

"You fixing to walk the whole way, are you?"

"My horse was stolen by Injuns. They took practically everything. My supplies, my guns, my water skin." Carter sniffled. "It was the last straw, King. A man can only take so much."

Nate slid down. The greenhorn was swaying and his hands shook as if with palsy. "Let me guess. You came west thinking you'd make your fortune in plews, and you struck off for the Rockies on your own?"

Carter nodded. His cheeks were slick with tears. "But you found out the hard way that trapping isn't all its cracked up to be. I'll bet you hardly caught any beaver."

"Just one," the man said, "and then I couldn't cure the damn hide right. It got all stiff and hard on me."

It was the same old story Nate had heard dozens of times, with minor variations. Back in the States, certain so-called journalists and other unscrupulous types were filling the heads of young men with all sorts of lies and half-truths about the glorious life of wealth and leisure awaiting anyone who spent just a few years trapping for a living. The fact was that free trappers never made more than enough to get by, while company trappers made a pittance.

The only ones who got rich off the fur trade were the heads of the big fur enterprises. But that was the way it had always been, in all facets of life. Those with money lorded it over those without, and arranged things so that more and more wealth flowed into their hands at the expense of honest hard-working souls who were trod under their financial heels. Or, to put it more succinctly, the rich stayed rich and the poor made them richer.

"You must be hungry," Nate declared, offering a piece of pemmican from his possibles bag.

Carter snatched it and bit off half in one bite. He chewed greedily, groaning all the while.

"Tell me," Nate coaxed, "when was the last time you had something to eat or drink?"

"I can't remember. I think it was three days ago."

"Then have a seat and I'll treat you to some of the best jerky this side of the Divide. My wife made it herself." Nate helped the greenhorn sit and stepped to his horse to open a parfleche.

"I don't know how to thank you, mister," Carter said, his voice quavering with emotion. "You have no idea the nightmare I've been through." He sniffled some more, louder than before. "To tell you the truth, I can't quite believe this is happening. I half think I'm dreaming this whole thing, that in a few minutes I'll wake up and find I've been chewing on grass or some such."

"Don't fret yourself. This coon is real enough." Nate gave him a half-dozen thick slices of jerky. "Your guardian angel must be watching over you, mister. Another day, and you would have keeled over and never gotten up again. You must be mighty tough to have made it this far."

The compliment had the opposite effect than Nate intended. Unexpectedly, Emmet Carter broke down and bawled like a distraught baby. He cried and cried, his face buried in his arms, blubbering and wheezing until he had cried himself dry. At length he wiped his nose with the back of a dirty sleeve and looked up. "I don't know how I'll ever be able to repay you for saving my life."

"You're not out of the woods yet, hoss. Were it up to me, I'd take you back to my cabin and fatten you up, give you a chance to regain your strength. Then in a month or so I'd escort you to Bent's Fort so you could hitch up with the next caravan back to Fort Leavenworth."

"You can't do that?" Carter asked, a forlorn note hinting at a sudden panic that salvation was about to be denied him. He glanced at the stallion, and for a moment it seemed as if he contemplated leaping erect and trying to ride off before Nate could stop him. But he stayed where he was.

Over the next several minutes Nate filled the man in about the Crows and the rescue mission to save Fetches Water.

The greenhorn listened intently, his mouth constantly crammed with jerky. "These Crows are friendly, you say?" he asked when the mountain man concluded.

"Friendly enough, although one or two of them would slit your throat as soon as look at you," Nate conceded. "But the only way out of the fix you're in is for you to throw in with us. Once we have the Crow girl safe, we can get you to William Bent, a friend of mine."

Emmet Carter never hesitated. "I don't have much choice, do I? Bring on the Crows, King."

So Nate did. Another council had to be held, conducted in sign for his benefit. The two troublemakers objected vigorously to having the greenhorn along, but Two Humps overruled them. So long as the man did not slow them down, the venerable leader had no objections. Nor did Bull Standing With Cow.

In an hour they were on their way, Carter riding double with Zach. The boy was glad to make the man's acquaintance. He had never met anyone from Maryland before and asked dozens of questions about the greenhorn's life there.

Nate and Winona overheard most of the talk. They learned that Carter was the son of a shoemaker, that he had balked at following in his father's footsteps and decided to strike off on his own. So he'd spent every last penny he had to outfit himself as a trapper and lit a shuck for parts unknown.

Winona was happy that her son and the stranger were getting along so well. She could not help but note that Carter acted ill at ease when close to any of the Crows, which she blamed on undue fear that he would be harmed.

That night the war party camped between two

knolls bordered by a ribbon of a stream. Supper consisted of antelope, a pronghorn He Dog dropped with an arrow at a range of 70 yards, a remarkable shot by any standard.

The men took turns standing guard. Nate had the last watch and got to see vivid bands of pink and yellow decorate the horizon as the sun made its advent known. He had coffee perking when the rest roused themselves from under their blankets.

Emmet Carter was like a new man that morning. The rest and the meals had done wonders for his constitution, and he chatted amiably with Zach from dawn until they fell asleep that night.

And so it went for three more otherwise uneventful days.

Nate got to know Carter better and regarded him as a decent enough young man who would make something of himself now that he knew riches never fell into one's lap like manna from heaven. He had learned the hard way that most people had to make ends meet through the sweat of their brow. Schemes to get rich quick only benefitted the schemers.

Then came the fifth day, and that evening Nate picked a site on a low bluff where scrub trees clustered thick around a small clear spring. While several Crows collected dead wood for the fire and Winona was busy preparing coffee, Nate took his son hunting. They descended the slope and bore to the east. Hardly had they rounded the end of the bluff when they spooked five does which bounded off, flashing the white undersides of their erect tails.

"Look, Pa!" Zach bellowed, giving chase. His pinto was fleet of foot, and in moments he was close enough to shoot. But drawing a bead from the back of a moving horse was hard to do. No sooner would Zach fix the sights squarely on a target than the deer would swerve or bound high into the air, spoiling the shot.

Nate stayed alongside his son. He refrained from firing to give Zach the practice. One of the does began to lag and he called out, "You have to think one step ahead of them. Aim high just as that last one starts to jump."

Zach let go of the reins and used his legs to guide the pinto, a Shoshone trick he had been taught when he was barely old enough to sit a horse. Wedging the stock tight against his shoulder, he sighted down the bobbing barrel, steadied his arms, and did exactly as his father had instructed him. He found that by aiming high, the deer bounded directly into his sights at the apex of each jump. All he had to do was adjust to its rhythm and stroke the trigger at just the right instant.

At the blast, the doe crumpled as if all four legs had been splintered. It slid to a stop and rolled onto its side, convulsing just once before it went limp with its tongue jutting out.

"I did it!" Zach cried, proud of his accomplishment. It was a first for him, a feat he could brag of when he visited the Shoshones and all the boys were bragging of special deeds they had done since last they were together.

Among most tribes, a man's prowess as a hunter was of critical importance. After all, no woman wanted to move into the lodge of a warrior famed for counting coup but who couldn't keep the supper pot supplied with a variety of game. Likewise, the quality of a warrior's clothes, the state of his lodge, and a great many other everyday items all depended on a steady supply of hides, bones, feathers and other bodily parts of various animals.

So Zach took almost as much joy in improving his hunting ability as he did in counting coup. He had learned a tactic that would serve him in good stead in the future.

Rather than butcher the doe on the spot, they threw it over the back of the stallion, then returned to camp. Bull Standing With Cow helped them skin the deer and cut the meat. Two Humps gave Winona a hand setting up a makeshift spit.

Soon everyone was gathered around the fire, waiting for their morsel. Emmet Carter sat near the Kings with his arms wrapped around his legs. He was unusually pensive, which Nate chalked up to fatigue since they had spent over ten hours on the go that day.

The venison was juicy and tasty. Nate treated himself to two helpings, and when he was done he licked his fingers clean and sat back to let the food digest.

Carter was still eating. He could never seem to get enough, gorging himself at every meal. Pausing to wipe his hands on his pants, he smiled at Nate and commented, "I want to thank you again for all you've done for me. I'll never forget it."

"Thank me when we get you to Bent's Fort, not before," Nate said.

"How long would that be, do you expect?"

"My best guess would be about a month yet," Nate said, "provided everything goes smoothly. Which it never does."

"A month," Carter said in transparent disappointment. "I hope you won't hold it against me if I think that's much too long to wait."

"Not at all. I don't blame you for wanting to get back sooner. After all you've been through, you're probably straining at the bit to head east."

"My sentiments exactly," Carter declared. "It's

nice to know we see eye to eye."

Nate didn't attach much significance to the conversation and turned to the cradleboard to spend time with his daughter. She laughed for joy as he played with her fingers and made silly faces. When she grew tired, Winona went off to feed her and Nate laid on his back with a forearm over his eyes to ward off the glare from the fire.

The trapper was more weary than he realized. He dozed off, awakening later when Winona threw a blanket over him and once more toward midnight when He Dog was giving another warrior a hard time about getting up and keeping watch. After the hothead complied, Nate drifted into dreamland, confident that Long Forelock would awaken him when it was his turn.

The yip of a coyote snapped Nate out of a sound sleep. He had the impression only an hour or so had gone by. Stretching, he observed that the fire had nearly burned itself out. That perplexed him. And his perplexity mounted when he turned his face to the heavens and realized the stars were all wrong. By their positions, it was much later than it should have been. In fact, dawn was less than an hour off.

Nate sat up. His wife and children slept soundly nearby. On the other side of the fire were seven Crows. The eighth had to be on watch.

Quietly rising, Nate sought some sign of the warrior. But there was none. He studied those who were sleeping and concluded that Long Forelock was the one missing. The obvious conclusion was that the Crow had gone off somewhere and dozed off.

Moving around the spring to the horses, Nate scoured the bluff in vain. Mystified, he walked to the end of the string. Suddenly it dawned on him that a horse was missing. He counted to be sure. It was Zach's pinto.

Now alarmed, Nate made a swift circuit of the camp. He saw no one and was going to awaken the others when he glimpsed a shadowy shape lying amid thick brush. Drawing a flintlock, he went over.

It was Long Forelock. The back of his skull had been caved in with a large rock, splitting it like an overripe melon and spilling his brains onto the ground. There was no consolation in the knowledge that the warrior had undoubtedly died instantly without being aware of what had happened.

An icy chill came over Nate as he walked back to the fire. The spot where Emmet Carter was supposed to be sleeping was bare. The greenhorn was gone, and a hasty check revealed he had swiped Winona's rifle, Zach's pistol, a blanket and a sizeable chunk of leftover deer meat with him.

Nate stood and stared eastward. He felt as if every lick of blood were draining from his body. "You damned fool," he said under his breath, and bowed his head, the enormous consequences of the greenhorn's treachery bearing down on his broad shoulders as if he were the mythical Atlas bearing the weight of the entire world.

After a while Nate stirred. He checked that his pistols were loaded before he saddled the stallion. Into a parfleche he packed enough jerky and pemmican to last him several days. As he was tying the straps, Two Humps rose on an elbow.

"Are you leaving us, Grizzly Killer?" the Crow signed.

Nate could think of no way to break the news gently. "The other white man has killed Long

Forelock and stolen the paint that belongs to my son."

In a twinkling Two Humps was on his feet. Nate led him to the body and stood back while the warrior knelt and clenched at the grass in impotent fury. When Two Humps calmed, he turned.

"I do not understand. How can he have done this? None of us mistreated him. Tell me *why*," he pleaded.

"I will know that when I catch him."

"And what will you do then?"

Nate merely looked at the body.

The others were waking up. Winona saw her husband approach and sensed right away that something was amiss. On hearing his account, she began to pack up their effects. "We will go with you," she said.

"No."

When two people have lived together day in and day out for years, they get to know one another as well as they do themselves. Nate's misery was like a physical force to Winona, a sword knifing deep into the depths of her soul. "You do not need to take this all on yourself."

"I was the one who insisted we lend him a helping hand. The blame is all mine."

Over half of the Crows agreed. He Dog and Runs Against and two others were outraged and all for pursuing Carter themselves. It took all of Two Humps's powers of persuasion to convince them to let Nate deal with the betrayer.

Young Zach was fit to be tied when the commotion woke him up and he learned about his pinto. "Why'd he take my horse?" he railed. "What did I ever do to him?"

"He took the paint because it was used to him," Nate answered. "He'd ridden it for days and knew it wouldn't act up when he threw on your saddle."

"The varmint," Zach snapped. "I'd like to get my hands on him!"

"Think again," Nate said, and stepped into the stirrups. His loved ones and the Crows were equally somber as he turned the stallion. "Head to the northeast for two days," he directed Winona. "I should rejoin you long before then, but if not, camp and wait for me."

"Take care, husband."

"Always."

Nate lifted the reins but paused when He Dog strode forward.

"Prove you are our friend, Grizzly Killer," the firebrand arrogantly signed. "Bring us the hair of your white brother and we will know that your words are not as empty as the air around us."

The stallion raised a swirl of dust as it trotted around the spring and on down the bluff. To the east a golden crown framed the plain, but there was only darkness in the heart of the man called Nate King.

Chapter Six

Winona King did not like the idea of being left alone with the Crows. But she made no protest when her husband rode off. She understood why he had to go. And she knew that Evelyn, Zach and she would slow him down. So she stoically accepted the fact and got on with the business at hand.

Nate had been out of sight but a few moments when Winona caught He Dog giving her a look that did not bode well. But it didn't worry her unduly. If trouble arose, she was confident she could count on Two Humps, Bull Standing With Cow and Flying Hawk to side with her.

Then, too, Winona was armed. Nate had given her his Hawken and she also had her pistol. She had demonstrated back at the cabin that she knew how to use a gun as well as any man, so He Dog would think twice before he tried anything.

Winona was eternally grateful to Nate for teaching her how to shoot. It permitted her to hold her own wherever she went.

Men, by virtue of their greater bulk and superior physical strength, tended to lord it over women. Even some in her own tribe liked to strut about as if they were bull elk at the height of rutting season, and in their lodges they treated their wives worse than they did their prized war horses.

At the annual rendezvous, there were always drunks to deal with. White men, Winona had learned, could be unspeakably wicked when they were under the influence of firewater. They often tried to force themselves on women who spurned their advances, causing fights to break out.

But no man, drunk or sober, white or red, would ever try to abuse a woman who could defend herself. A flintlock enabled a woman to compensate for her smaller size and put her on equal footing with any man. With a gun she could assert herself and stand up to those brutish males who would inflict suffering on anyone weaker than they were.

It was a King family custom for Nate to read to them several times a week. Once, years ago, during one such session, Nate had mentioned that certain wise men among his people had put on paper a list of all those things which were crucial to the welfare of white men and women everywhere.

Near the top of that list, Nate had told her, was the right to bear arms. It was not to be denied any citizen, as the whites called themselves. Those wise men had known that those who could not defend themselves were virtual slaves to those who had power over them. Winona had been much impressed by their wisdom.

An added factor that helped ease Winona's

mind about her husband's departure was the presence of their son. Stalking Coyote was young, true, but he had counted coup. He had slain enemies in the heat of battle, and would leap to her defense if any of the Crows acted up.

Zach was prepared to do just that. Astride Long Forelock's horse, he stayed close to his mother all morning. If He Dog or Runs Against rode anywhere near them, he was quick to heft his rifle and glare until the warriors fell back with the others.

Two Humps and Bull Standing With Cow were another story. The warriors took turns spending time with the Kings. Zach figured the Crows liked their company, but his mother was more astute. Winona knew it was their way of forestalling trouble. He Dog and Runs Against were not about to bother her when the older warriors were present.

Noon found them miles from the bluff, resting the horses at an isolated stand of trees.

The spring day was cool with a brisk breeze. Winona gave pemmican to Zach, then ambled to the opposite side of the stand and sat with her back to a tree to feed her daughter. She laid the heavy Hawken across her thighs and made herself comfortable.

It was quiet and peaceful there. The serenity, combined with the soft rustle of leaves overhead and the pleasant sensation of Evelyn's sucking, induced Winona to doze. Minutes went by.

Suddenly the feeling of pressure on Winona's legs vanished. She sat bolt upright and was stunned to discover the rifle was gone.

Standing to her right, holding the Hawken loosely in one hand with his other resting on the hilt of his long butcher knife, was He Dog. Smirking, he leaned the rifle against a sapling just out of her reach, then signed, "Did you lose something, woman?"

"Do you always play games more fit for children?" Winona retorted. She casually covered her breast without disturbing Evelyn, who slumbered on her chest. As she lowered her arm she contrived to place her hand close to the butt of her pistol without the Crow noticing.

"It seems to me, Shoshone," He Dog signed, "that you have never learned your proper place. It is not fitting for a woman to show disrespect to a warrior."

"Nor does a true warrior show disrespect to a woman," Winona said, refusing to be cowed.

He Dog ignored her comment. "You should never have taken a white man as your husband. Whites do not know how to treat their women. They are too soft on them."

"Be sure to tell that to Grizzly Killer when he returns. I want to see the look on your face when my soft husband beats you senseless as he did back at our wooden lodge."

A scarlet tinge flushed He Dog's cheeks, and he took a half step toward her. "If you were mine, I would soon teach you to hold your tongue."

Winona smiled sweetly and put as much venom in her tone as she could muster. "Crow, I would not be your woman if you were the only man left alive."

"You are Shoshone. What do you know? Any Crow woman would be proud to live in my lodge."

A thought struck Winona and she signed, "Question. Do you have a wife yet? Or are Crow women as smart as I think they are?"

He Dog bristled and bent to seize her. He rooted himself in place when her pistol blossomed as if by magic, the muzzle so close to his face that he was staring into the barrel.

Winona motioned and the warrior slowly backed off. She set the flintlock on her lap and signed, "Never, ever lay a finger on me, Crow. I will not go easy on you as my husband did for Two Humps's sake."

"Your husband is a fool. He should have rubbed me out while he had the chance," He Dog responded. "No man puts a hand on a Crow and lives to brag of it. I have held back because Bull Standing With Cow has asked me to." The stocky warrior leaned toward her, his swarthy visage aglow with fiery spite. "But know this, Shoshone. Once we have rescued Fetches Water, I will hold back no longer. Your precious white man will pay. And you will be in need of a new husband."

So signing, He Dog spun and stomped off, his spine as stiff as the trees around them.

Winona shivered. Whether from the cool breeze or the threat, she couldn't rightly say. He Dog was not to be taken lightly. For all his faults, he was a man of his word. He planned to kill Nate, and nothing would stop him short of his own death.

Brush close by shook as if to the passage of a small animal. Or a man on hands and knees. Thinking that the Crow had circled around to take her by surprise, Winona put a hand on her pistol just as the brush parted to reveal her protector.

Zach strolled into the open, his cocked pistol out. "If he'd kept it up, I aimed to put a ball into him," he stated. His father had long ago made it plain that when his father was gone, he was the man of the family. Safeguarding his mother and sister was a responsibility he took seriously.

"Were you spying on him the whole time?"

"Sure was," Zach confided. "I never let him out of my sight. Runs Against is another bad apple, but He Dog is the worst of the two."

"You heard what he said. I think we are safe until after we find Bull Standing With Cow's daughter."

"Never take anything for granted where your enemies are concerned," Zach quoted. "Isn't that what Pa is always telling us?"

It was. Winona smiled as she tucked Evelyn into the cradleboard. At moments like these her son reminded her so much of Nate that it was as if he were a smaller version of her husband. He helped hoist the cradleboard onto her back and handed her the Hawken. "Thank you," she said. In a good mood for the first time that day, she headed for the war party.

"I wonder how Pa is faring?" Zach remarked.

Just like that, Winona's fine spirits evaporated. "We'll know soon enough," was all she would say.

At that very moment the man they were both anxious about was bearing eastward at a steady trot. Since daybreak Nate King had held the stallion to a brisk pace in the hope that he would overtake Emmet Carter before the day was done. But as time passed he acknowledged that it might be wishful thinking on his part.

The greenhorn was pushing the pinto mercilessly. They had not stopped once, near as Nate could tell. If Carter kept on the way he was doing, the poor horse would play out on him in a day or two. Until then, the trapper had to content himself with sticking to the trail and trying not to worry about his loved ones.

To occupy himself, Nate tried to imagine what sort of man would betray his trust the way the greenhorn had. He'd done all in his power on the Easterner's behalf, and look at how Carter had repaid him!

The younger man's upbringing probably had something to do with it, Nate reflected. From what he had learned, Carter's folks had pampered him when he was little. They'd never made him do chores or work at odd jobs to earn money on his own. Consequently he'd come to think that anything he wanted should be his for the taking. Carter had been spoiled to the extent that he figured life owed him a living when actually it was the other way around.

But the greenhorn's lazy parents were only partly to blame. Carter had to shoulder a large measure of the fault for never growing past the selfish stage most younguns went through. There came a time when any growing boy had to accept full responsibility for his acts. Those who never learned this most important of all lessons went through life, as Nate's grandmother had once phrased it, "as brats in men's clothing."

Emmet Carter wanted to go home. So he figured that meant he had the right to do whatever he liked to achieve his goal. Killing was justified because it was in his own best interests. Stealing was acceptable because he needed what he stole. There was no ironclad right or wrong, in his eyes. He did as he pleased without regard for anyone else.

Nate had known men like Carter before, mainly during the years he'd spent growing up in New York. City life, he'd observed, tended to breed selfish individuals much as alleys and basements and tunnels bred rats. He suspected that it had something to do with the fact that in cities, men and women had all their wants met simply by handing over a few dollars or a handful of coins. They never had to hunt game for their supper or for hides to make clothes. They never had to go without so long as they earned enough to make ends meet.

In the country it was different. Rural folk not only had to earn a living, they had to butcher animals for food and cure pelts for clothes and do a hundred and one other things that city dwellers wouldn't think of doing. Country folk were more in touch with the world around them, more in harmony with the cycles of nature and basic survival.

Nate's mentor, Shakespeare McNair, claimed that one day there would be more city dwellers than country dwellers. Nate hoped he wasn't around to see that happen. The day it did, America would cease to be a country of basically honest, hard-working people who respected others as they respected themselves, and become a nation of selfish individuals who were always looking out for their own interests before all else.

Shaking his head to dispel his train of thought, Nate buckled down to tracking. For the better part of the afternoon he pressed on through the high grass. He lost count of the number of rabbits he spooked and the number of frightened prairie chickens that took wing. Deer were common. So were roving coyotes and packs of wolves, which gave him a wide berth.

About three o'clock Nate rode over a low rise and came on a fair-sized herd of buffalo. The snort of a bull was all it took to stampede the huge brutes southward. He reined up until the last of them were gone, then swung wide of the choking cloud of dust they had raised.

The herd had trampled the grass to bits and their flying hooves had torn up the ground in spots, erasing Carter's trail. Nate had to hunt for a while before he found it again, losing valuable time in the process.

Well before sunset Nate foresaw that he wouldn't catch up with the greenhorn that day. He slowed to a walk the last hour and stopped for the night in a buffalo wallow, where he got a small fire going. His meal consisted of jerky and pemmican.

Before turning in, Nate walked to a nearby hillock and scanned the prairie ahead. No telltale glow gave Carter away this time. Either the man was learning from his mistakes, he hadn't bothered with a fire, or he was farther ahead than Nate counted on.

The big trapper slept fitfully. He kept dreaming of Winona, Zach and Evelyn, and imagining them in all kinds of peril. Well before the sun brightened the sky he was in the saddle, taking up the chase again.

It was the middle of the morning when Nate located the spot where Carter had spent the night. The greenhorn had stumbled on a spring and shot a rabbit. So both the man and his mount were refreshed and raring to go. Catching them would be harder than ever.

Nate rode on. So accustomed was he to always having his Hawken at hand that it felt strange to be without it for once. He still had the pair of polished smoothbore flintlocks, but they were only reliable at short range.

Shortly before noon a brown hump appeared a few hundred feet to the northeast. At first Nate mistook it for a solitary buffalo, but as he drew nearer the creature heard the stallion and reared up onto its hind legs.

It was an enormous grizzly. The mighty carnivore rumbled an ominous warning, its gaping maw wide, its giant paws cleaving the air as if it were eager to do the same to the mountain man.

Nate never slowed but he did swing to the south. The monster watched him closely, and he feared that it might drop onto all fours and charge before he was a safe distance away. Grizzlies were as fleet as horses over short distances; he'd seen one topple a Shoshone warrior from a mount moving at a breakneck gallop.

Suddenly the bear sank back down. The hump on its broad shoulders was the only part of it that Nate could see. The grizzly moved in his direction, then inexplicably changed course, hastened westward, and was soon lost to view.

Nate stayed alert. Where there was one bear, there were sometimes more. Relaxing was out of the question until he had put two miles behind him.

He had lost more time. Not much, but enough to insure that Emmet Carter would elude him a second day.

Night caught Nate in the open. He made a cold camp, picketed the stallion, and curled up under a blanket with his arm for a pillow. It must have been two in the morning when a light sprinkle of cold raindrops fell, enough to awaken him and give him the chills. The rest of the night he tossed and turned.

Stiff and bedraggled, Nate rose at sunrise. He ate on the go, a handful of pemmican which barely sufficed to satisfy his gnawing hunger.

An hour later the trapper crossed a gully. Under an earthen overhang were the glowing embers of Carter's fire. Scattered feathers showed that the greenhorn had eaten his fill of prairie hen.

Nate was encouraged by the fact that he was only an hour behind his quarry. Apparently Carter believed that he had gotten clean away because the tracks were spaced much closer together; he was holding the pinto to a rapid walk.

Raking the stallion with his heels, Nate did the opposite. From time to time he rose in the stirrups to scan the prairie ahead. The thrill of success sent a tingle down his back when at long last he beheld an ant-sized figure almost on the horizon.

"Got you," Nate said softly to himself. He reduced his pace by half to maintain the distance between them. It would be unwise to let Carter spot him just yet. He had to sneak close enough to overhaul the greenhorn in a burst of speed.

All went well until noon. Nate kept the man in sight without giving himself away. Then a few low hills appeared, and Carter rode to the top of one and stopped. It was too far for Nate to see clearly, but it was evident the greenhorn had spotted him. The pinto wheeled and streaked on down the hill as if fleeing a prairie fire.

There was no recourse for Nate but to ride flat out. He wound through the hills rather than up and over them and saw Carter about half a mile distant.

Nate was a seasoned judge of horseflesh. He'd picked the pinto for his son because the animal had three qualities he admired most in a horse: a calm disposition, stamina, and speed. Now those same qualities were being displayed to his detriment, since the pinto was proving every bit as hardy as his own stallion. He gained ground, but not much.

Presently a long line of trees testified to the presence of a stream. Carter gained cover. Nate tried to keep him in sight but couldn't. He kept going and was well out from the cottonwoods when something tugged at the top of his beaver hat a fraction of a second before the sharp retort of the rifle wafted across the plain.

Instantly Nate slanted to the north and executed a trick taught him by a Shoshone warrior named Drags The Rope. He swung lithely onto the off-side of the stallion so that only his forearm and one foot showed. By peeking under the big black's neck, he guided it toward undergrowth less than 200 yards from the point where Carter had disappeared.

Nate thought he had thwarted the greenhorn, but he was wrong. Another shot rang out. The ball whizzed within inches of the stallion's head. Carter was trying to kill it! he realized, and swung back up. Bent low, he zigzagged for sanctuary.

Only one other shot boomed before Nate reached the undergrowth. There should have been two or three. Either Carter was as slow as molasses at reloading or he was conserving his ammo.

As tall weeds and trees closed around him, Nate straightened. To the left grew a thicket. Behind it he reined up and ground-hitched the stallion. Drawing both pistols, he edged to the east until he came to the stream, another wide but shallow waterway called different names by different tribes. The Shoshones referred to it as White Bark Creek, as Nate recollected.

Easing into the water, Nate hugged the bank and moved to the southeast. His intent was to catch Carter in the strip of vegetation between the stream and the prairie. Soon he came to a deep pool formed by a large tree that had fallen ages ago, partially blocking the flow. The water rose to his knees, then his waist. Since it wouldn't do to risk getting the pistols wet, he sought a suitable place to climb out.

That was when the brush above the bank crack-led.

Nate pressed flush with the bank and crouched so that only his head and his hands were above water. He heard footsteps, then a muttered oath.

"Damn it! Where the hell did he get to?"

Emmet Carter's shadow materialized on the surface of the pool. Nate couldn't see the green-horn, even though the man was so close he could hear Carter breathing. The shadow shifted, and Nate was positive that the man had his back to the stream. He cautiously rose to his full height and extended both pistols, sure the man had blundered right into his clutches.

But Carter was gone.

Nate scanned the pool but there was no trace of his shadow. He lifted a foot and scraped it along the bank, seeking purchase. There was none. The mud was as slick as bear fat.

Retracing his steps to a spot where the bank had crumpled leaving a wide cleft, Nate gingerly climbed a slippery incline. He paused every few seconds to scour the trees, but it was as if the earth had swallowed Carter up. Hunkering, he moved into a patch of high weeds and lowered onto his belly.

Nate had to adjust his strategy to compensate for the advantage the stolen rifle gave Carter. The man could fire at him from a long way off, while he had to wait until Carter was within 60 feet of his position, preferably less.

Not so much as a sparrow stirred anywhere. The shots had either scared the wild creatures off or silenced them, which worked in Nate's favor. He could hear faint noises better. And any movement he spied would more than likely be the greenhorn slinking along.

Soon something did move, in cottonwoods to the west. A flash of white and black hide revealed where Zach's pinto had been hidden. Nate started to crawl toward it. As he emerged from the weeds the horse let out a loud whinny, which was answered by another horse. But it wasn't Nate's stallion.

Whipping around, the trapper was startled to see five Indians nearing White Bark Creek from the east. Lured by the shots, they had come to investigate. They were well armed and had fanned out.

Even worse, they were Lakotas.

Chapter Seven

Two days of travel brought the war party to Red Willow Creek. They concealed themselves deep in a band of timber and kept a constant watch on the surrounding prairie.

As well they should. The place where they camped was less than 40 miles from the junction of the South Platte River with the Platte itself, where Nate had anticipated they would find the Oglalas encamped at that time of year.

It had been Nate's idea not to follow the South Platte all the way from the Rockies to where it merged with the larger Platte. His reasoning had been that they were more likely to encounter Sioux along the river, so he had stuck to the open plain. He'd outlined his strategy to Winona prior to leaving their cabin, and she'd agreed with it.

Now, deep in the heart of Lakota country with her young son and small daughter, Winona wished her man was at her side. She tried not to worry, but he had assured her that he would rejoin them well before the end of the second day. Sunset was not far off, yet he hadn't appeared.

To complicate matters, the Crows were restless. Being in the heart of enemy territory had put them all on edge. He Dog was the worst of the bunch. He paced like a trapped animal and snapped at his companions when addressed.

Even Two Humps wasn't immune. Many times he walked to a high stump at the edge of the clearing and climbed onto it to survey the sea of grass to the south. After the fifth time, he came over to where Winona rested with her children. "Where is he?" the warrior signed. "He should have been here by now."

"Grizzly Killer advised us to wait," Winona reminded him, "so that is what we will do."

"But for how long?" Two Humps asked. "You know as well as I do that the longer we stay here, the greater the chance of our being discovered."

Bull Standing With Cow had been watching the exchange. "If the Lakotas spot us, they will rouse every warrior in the tribe. We will be chased all the way back to the Shining Mountains." His features saddened. "I will never see my daughter again."

"We must be patient," Winona stressed. "It is unlikely the Oglalas will come across us. We are too well hidden." She gestured at Red Willow Creek. "There is plenty of water and grass for the horses, and we have enough pemmican to last several more sleeps."

He Dog stomped up. "I, for one, do not intend to stay here that long. Even if we do not make a fire, the Lakotas might find us. All it would take is for one of our horses to nicker when a war party or a band of hunters is passing by, or for the wind to shift."

Runs Against grunted in agreement.

Outwardly calm but simmering inside, Winona said, "Are we so helpless that we cannot cover the muzzles of our horses when Lakotas are near? As for the wind, we are too deep in the trees for it to carry off much of our scent." She paused and gave He Dog a haughty glance. "If I, a *woman*, am not afraid of the Lakotas, why should you be?"

The stocky warrior thumped his chest and responded, "I am not afraid of the Lakotas or anyone else!"

"Prove it," Winona shot back. Then, cradling Evelyn, she gently rocked her daughter and refrained from looking at the Crows. One by one they drifted off until only Two Humps remained. She raised her head.

The leader was smiling. "You are wise beyond your years, my Shoshone friend," he said, "and as sly as a fox."

Winona grinned, balanced the cradleboard on her legs, and replied, "Women learned long ago to rely on their wits when dealing with men." Her grin broadened. "In a battle of minds, most men are unarmed."

Two Humps started to rock with laughter but caught himself and walked off chuckling.

A few feet away, Zach leaned against his saddle, his rifle propped at his side. He admired the clever manner in which his mother had handled the situation and commented as much.

"We are not out of the woods yet," Winona said, resorting to a figure of speech her husband often used. "He Dog will pout until his patience is at an end, then he will cause more trouble. The next time, I might not be able to stop him from going off to find the Oglala village where Fetches Water is being held."

"He's a damn jackass," Zach stated before he could stop himself. Flustered, he hastily blurted, "Sorry, Ma. I didn't mean to use such strong language in front of you."

"I have heard stronger, Stalking Coyote," Winona said. "My ears will not fall off." She slid her daughter from the cradleboard and playfully held her in the air while giving a little shake. The child giggled and pumped her legs as if anxious to walk.

The Crows were huddled in two groups. In one was Two Humps, Bull Standing With Cow and Flying Hawk. The other included He Dog, Runs Against, Bear Ears and Yellow Owl.

Zach stretched. He opened a parfleche and helped himself to a strip of jerky. It was the first food he had eaten all day. Although he would not let on to his mother, he was so concerned about his father that it had spoiled his appetite. "I've been thinking," he mentioned between bites. "If Pa isn't back by nightfall, do you want to go look for him?"

Winona was of half a mind to consent but she answered, "Your father can take care of himself. We will do as he asked us and stay put until he catches up."

"But what if—" Zach began, stopping when his mother raised a hand.

"When you have lived as long as I have, my son, you will learn not to worry so much. Most of the time the things we worry about never happen. As your father likes to say, take one day at a time."

"That's easier said than done."

Winona nodded. She stared off to the south, careful not to let her son see the burning anxiety that blazed like twin bonfires in her eyes. *My husband*, she thought, where are you?

Nate King froze on spying the Lakotas. He had no idea if they were Oglalas, Minniconjous, San Arcs, Brules, or Hunkpapas. It didn't much matter. All Lakotas were hostile to whites. If they saw him, they'd try to make wolf meat of him.

The Sioux were scouring the west side of White Bark Creek. A tall warrior in the middle of the group abruptly pointed to the south with his lance and spoke a few words. In the blink of an eye the five warriors dashed off, entering the water further down and splashing across into a cluster of saplings.

Rising into a crouch, Nate ran toward his son's pinto. He no longer cared about Emmet Carter; the greenhorn was on his own. Nate had to get out of there before the Lakotas returned.

The paint stood with its head hung low, close to exhaustion. Its legs and sides were flecked with dirt, its body caked with dust. It snorted when Nate grabbed the reins and untied them from a tree limb, but once it sniffed at his arm the pinto let him lead it northward.

Nate was halfway to the thicket when a piercing shriek prickled the hair at the nape of his neck. Halting behind cottonwoods, he saw the greenhorn burst from the saplings the Sioux had gone into. Carter hobbled as he ran, an arrow jutting from high on his thigh. Panic etched his countenance.

On his heels came the five warriors. They were in no particular hurry. Two of them bore to the left, two others to the right, to hem him in, while the tall warrior with several eagle feathers in his hair followed the greenhorn into the creek.

Whining in pathetic terror, Emmet Carter spun and trained the rifle on the tall warrior. The Lakota stopped and sat calmly, a bow in his right hand with an arrow notched to the sinew string.

"Leave me be!" Carter cried. "Just turn tail and go or you'll be sorry!"

The bluff didn't work. The warriors simply stared at him, waiting.

"I mean it!" Carter yelled shrilly. "So help me God, I'll drop the first one who so much as lifts a finger against me!"

None of the Indians moved a muscle. Nate dared not move, himself, or they might spot him. He had to stand there and watch the tableau unfold. Carter's plight elicited no sympathy. The man had brought it down on his own head; he would have to reap the consequences.

Several of the Lakotas were smirking. This was sport to them. Rough, grim sport, to be sure, but the kind they enjoyed the most.

A hefty specimen armed with a lance edged his war horse closer and poked the tapered tip at Carter. He was having fun, not really trying to connect.

Carter misconstrued. "I warned you!" he wailed. Elevating the rifle, he stroked the trigger.

At the blast, the hefty warrior toppled from his horse, landing on his backside in waist-deep water. The ball had caught him well up on the right shoulder, passing under his collarbone. Dazed, he reached up and touched a finger to the trickle of blood seeping from the wound.

The lighthearted mood of the Sioux was gone. Their faces cast in flinty lines, they slowly closed in on the greenhorn.

"Damn you! Stay back!" Carter howled, clawing his stolen pistol free. Slowly back-pedaling, he swung the flintlock first at one warrior, then at another, trying to cover all four of them at the same time. "I'll shoot the next one of you in the head! Just see if I don't!"

His railing had no impact on the Lakotas. They continued to move toward him, although none, as yet, lifted a weapon.

Carter was on the verge of hysterics. "I know about you filthy savages!" he screamed. "I've heard the stories! And if you think I'll let you torture me, you have another think coming!" Shifting, he scanned the woods and called out in desperation, "King! Nate King! I know you're there somewhere! If you can hear me, I'm sorry for what I did! I just wanted to get home! Please help me! Together we can fight these bastards off!"

Nate frowned. Now the warriors knew there was another white man nearby. They were scanning the trees, and one was making for the west bank. Nate would have shot the greenhorn himself, but he needed both pistols primed for when the Sioux came after him.

"Answer me, damn it!" Carter screeched. "You can't just let these butchers rub me out! I'm white, like you. You can't stand by and let them kill me!"

The warrior on the west bank was peering into every shadow, checking behind every bush.

Nate had to act. Taking a single stride, he vaulted onto the pinto and took off like a bat out of hell to the north. Wolfish yips told him the Lakotas had spotted him. He looked back just as the tall warrior, in a blur, streaked the bow up and unleashed a shaft that transfixed Carter's right arm. The greenhorn screamed and dropped the pistol into the water. Two Sioux promptly rode him down.

That was all Nate had a chance to see. The warrior on the west bank was flying toward him, a lance upraised to hurl. Nate goaded the tired pinto on and was almost to the thicket when the Sioux drew within throwing range.

Twisting, Nate extended his left flintlock. The .55-caliber bucked and boomed, and the warrior catapulted backwards over the rump of his mount. Cries of outrage issued from the Lakotas as he jammed the spent piece under his belt.

Speeding to the stallion, Nate scooped up the reins and fled. His only hope lay in outdistancing them. Body bent low, he trotted to the northwest and within moments laid eyes on the prairie. And more Lakotas. Seven or eight warriors were rapidly bearing down on the cottonwoods.

Cutting back to the right, Nate rode parallel with White Bark Creek. He stuck to dense brush and covered 50 yards without being seen. Then a bellow warned him that the Sioux were in hard pursuit. The pinto was doing its best, but it was on its last legs. He would be better off on the stallion, but there was no time to switch.

Arrows whizzed down around him. Most were wide of the mark, but a few missed him by a hand's width. He veered farther to the right and plowed through high weeds to find himself almost at the edge of the creek bank. Legs pumping, he flew northward.

Sioux were surging toward the big trapper from the rear and from the left. Their war whoops and yips formed a harsh chorus, which grew louder as they narrowed the gap.

Nate was swiftly losing ground. The pinto just was not up to a sustained chase. Hauling hard on the stallion's reins, he guided the big black up alongside the smaller paint. Girding himself, he raised his legs and tucked them up under him. It was difficult to keep his balance, but he managed.

More arrows sought his life as Nate coiled and sprang to the left. For a dizzying moment he hung suspended in the air between the two horses, and for a harrowing instant it seemed as if he would drop straight down and be trampled. Then he alighted on the stallion, clamped his legs tight, and reluctantly allowed the pinto to slow to a walk even as he brought the stallion to a pell-mell gallop.

The Lakotas erupted in baffled yells. Two of them gave up their pursuit to catch the paint, but the rest rode faster than ever.

Nate swiveled. There was no sign of Emmet Carter. He figured the man was a goner, and he was determined not to suffer the same fate. With the stallion under him, he at least had a prayer of eluding the Sioux.

White Bark Creek wound to the left, so Nate bore to the right. Cold water soaked his moccasins and the bottom of his leggings as he angled into the water and barreled for the other shore.

From out of nowhere hurtled a warrior. The man had a fusee, a trade rifle given to Indians for two to three times its value in prime plews. He pointed it and squeezed the trigger but nothing happened. The gun misfired. Undaunted, the Lakota wielded the fusee as he might a club.

Pulling his other pistol, Nate shot the warrior squarely in the forehead. The Sioux fell into the creek with a tremendous splash. The riderless horse halted. Seconds later Nate gained the top of the far bank and hurried into the trees before the bowmen could get his range.

Over ten Lakotas swarmed into the water, each eager to be the one who counted first coup.

Both Nate's flintlocks were empty. Since it was

next to impossible to reload on the fly, he shoved the second one under his belt so his hands would be free for handling the reins. Bit by bit he widened his lead.

Even if Nate got away, his problems were just beginning. Thanks to Carter, the Lakotas were alerted to the presence of enemies in their country. War parties would be sent out from every village. Soon the territory would be swarming with hostiles. The Crows and his family would be lucky if they got out alive.

The tree line appeared. Once past it Nate would rely on the stallion's superior endurance to save his bacon. A glance over a shoulder revealed the nearest warriors were not quite close enough to let their arrows fly.

In no time, glistening grass enclosed him. Nate spied a ridge to the east and made for it. The stallion's brief rest had rekindled its customary vigor, and it was flowing over the ground with a smooth, powerful gait.

When next Nate checked, the Lakotas were so far behind, their bows were useless. His confidence growing, he smiled and began to plot how best to rejoin his family. Quite clearly he would have to do most of his traveling at night, laying low in ravines and gullies during the day.

Inexplicably, the Sioux commenced hollering and howling as if they were demented wolves. This went on and on, without letup.

Unable to comprehend why and thinking it might be a ruse, Nate watched them closely. They were spreading out wider than ever, a pointless act in his estimation, since they had no hope of overtaking him. One of them had a rifle which he pointed at the clouds and fired off.

It made no sense.

Then an answering shot sounded on the ridge, and Nate faced front to discover another dozen or so warriors on the crest. Already they were fanning out, too, working in concert with the Lakotas behind him.

"Damn!" Nate exploded, wheeling the stallion to the south. He had almost made a fatal error.

The warriors to the west were trying to head him off. Several were well out ahead of the main pack and smacking their quirts against their mounts like men possessed. Those on the ridge were farther away, but the slope lent them speed as they poured down onto the flatland.

Nate checked to verify his knife was still in its sheath. If they caught him, he was not going to go down without a fight. There would be none of the useless posturing Carter had done. It would be do or die time, as the saying went.

The stallion, as always, responded superbly. Few horses were its equal, as it demonstrated to the Lakotas by racing beyond the reach of those about to close the trap.

An arrow flashed in front of Nate's face. The lean warrior responsible quickly began to notch another shaft but stopped at a shout from a fellow Sioux. Yet a third man was about to throw a lance but lowered the weapon instead.

Nate did not like that one bit. It meant they wanted to take him alive, and their only reason for doing so would be to torture him at their leisure later on.

Some tribes, like the Apaches, were known to relish inflicting torment on captives. Often it was done to test the mettle of their enemies. Those who held up well, who did not whimper or plead for mercy, were usually accorded a quick death to honor their bravery. But those who caved in were treated to even worse abuse; they could scream and beg all they wanted and all their captors would do was laugh at them.

The Blackfeet were notorious for torturing trappers. They had a long-standing grudge against white men which stemmed from a clash between members of the Lewis and Clark expedition and several warriors.

According to the stories Nate had heard, the Lakotas were not as partial to torture. At least, they were known to adopt captive women and children into their tribe and treat them as if they were full-blooded Sioux. Male captives, though, were seldom so fortunate.

The pounding of hooves resembled the din of a buffalo stampede. Swirling clouds of smoke rose in the wake of the Lakotas. Their long hair whipped in the wind, lending them the aspect of a horde of painted demons.

Suddenly the terrain itself turned against Nate. A wide gully appeared before him. He had no other option but to slow briefly as he negotiated the steep slope. Then he bore to the left and sped madly around a bend and along a straight stretch rife with dry brush and loose earth.

The Lakotas were elated. Their yells rose to the clouds as they pursued him along the rim.

Nate earnestly sought some way up out of the gully on the other side. But the slope was too sheer for the stallion to climb, perhaps too sheer for a man to scale.

Praying that there would be a break in the wall somewhere, Nate rushed around a sharp turn to the southeast and saw one. Only it was on the same side as the Lakotas. No sooner did he thunder past it than a quartet of warriors reached the gully floor.

Trail's End

The stallion picked that moment to stumble. Nate was nearly unhorsed as its head jerked low and its hind quarters rose in a bounding hop. He was able to stay on, but it had given the warriors an opportunity they were quick to take advantage of.

Lakotas were on both sides, so close they could reach out and touch him. One on the right did, trying to snag his arm, but Nate tore free and swung a backhand blow that missed.

The warrior on the other side instantly lunged and caught hold of Nate's leg. Nate felt himself start to spill to the right. Spinning at the waist, he slammed a fist into the Sioux's elbow and the man released him. But the very next second the warrior on the right attempted once again to seize a limb.

Constantly swinging back and forth, Nate held them at bay. He couldn't do so, however, and hold the big black to a gallop. Gradually he slowed, which turned out to be just the thing the Lakotas were waiting for.

A third Sioux pressed in close behind the stallion. In his one hand he held a coiled length of buffalo hide rope. In the other he gripped a small noose which he now swung rapidly in a tight circle.

Nate noticed the man, but most of his attention was claimed by the pair trying to pluck him from his saddle. The brave on the left swooped in closer than ever. Turning, Nate arced back his fist to land a solid punch.

With a deft flip, the third Lakota sent the small noose sailing neatly over Nate's hand. The buffalo hide settled around his wrist, constricting when the warrior gave the rope a stiff tug. Nate tensed every muscle in his arm to resist the rope's pull, but it was a lost cause. Especially when the war-

101

rior brought his mount to a sliding stop.

There was a terrible spasm in Nate's shoulder, and he became airborne. Yanked clear off the stallion, he saw the earth rushing up to meet his face. The pain was exquisite. Marshaling his wits, he struggled to sit up and tear the rope off, but before he could the sky seemed to rain Lakotas, warrior after warrior pouncing on top of him until they bore him down by the sheer weight of their numbers.

Nate's last conscious sensation was of a tremendous blow to the head. Then a black void engulfed him.

Chapter Eight

Wi-No-Na of the Shoshones woke up with a start. She had been having a terrible dream in which her husband was being slowly strangled by a dozen pair of brawny hands at once. She had not seen the faces or even the bodies of his killers, only those awful hands.

Profoundly disturbed, Winona rose onto her elbows. Beside her in the cradleboard slept little Blue Flower, as beautiful as only a sleeping child could be. Nearby lay Stalking Coyote, his rifle at his side. Across the fire dozed the Crows, except for Bull Standing With Cow, who was keeping watch. He had moved off a score of feet and sat on the stump with his back to the low fire.

Rising, Winona pulled her blanket tight around her slender shoulders and walked over to him. The aged warrior looked up at her, his features as sorrowful as any she had ever seen. There was no need to ask what he had been thinking about.

"You are up early," the Crow signed.

Winona shrugged.

Bull Standing With Cow gazed off into the darkness to the south of their camp. "I understand. I am very worried about your husband also. He should have rejoined us by now."

"He promised us he would catch up and he will."

The warrior sighed. "Is that your head talking or your heart? We both know that nothing short of death would keep him from your side. I am afraid that if he does not show by sunset today, we must fear the worst."

"I will never give up hope."

"As well you should not," Bull Standing With Cow signed. "You are a credit to your man. In many ways you remind me of my own woman when she was much younger. I trust your Grizzly Killer knows how lucky he is?"

Winona changed the subject. "One more day of delay will not make much difference. But you saw He Dog earlier. He will not want to sit around here much longer. How do you propose to control him?"

"Control He Dog?" Bull Standing With Cow said, and chuckled softly. "I might as well try to control a great brown bear or a mad bull buffalo. No one can tell him what to do. At best, we can try to convince him that it is better for everyone if we lay low for a while longer. Whether he will agree is impossible to predict."

"You should not have brought him."

"I knew it was not a smart thing to do," the Crow admitted, "but I was desperate. Of all the warriors who survived the Lakota attack, only nine agreed to go with me. I could not afford to refuse him."

He paused. "And there was another factor I had to take into account."

Winona's female intuition served her in good stead. "Your daughter?" she guessed.

Bull Standing With Cow blinked. "Yes. He Dog has shown an interest in her for some time. Soon she will be eligible, and I expect he will court her."

"How does Fetches Water feel about him?"

"She never told me. She has always been a quiet girl who keeps her innermost thoughts to herself." The devoted father smiled wanly. "But then, most women do, don't they? Long ago I learned that women are much better at keeping secrets than men are. And I think I know why that is."

"This I would like to hear."

"It is simple. Women protect their hearts with the same devotion a man will protect his loved ones or his best war horse. Women place more value on that which takes place inside of them, while men place more value on things they can see, touch, and hold."

Winona grinned. "You are very wise—for a man."

They both laughed lightly, and for a few moments the father's sadness was gone. But it returned the instant he stopped. He wearily rubbed his eyes, then stifled a yawn.

"If I do not get some rest soon, I will not be good for anything. But I am so worried about my daughter that I can hardly eat or sleep."

Sunrise was over an hour off. Winona put a hand on his shoulder and offered, "If you want to get some rest now, I will stand watch for you."

"I would like to, but what would the others think?"

"They know how hard you have been pushing yourself," Winona noted. "I will be right back."

She fetched the Hawken and Evelyn and perched on the stump with the cradleboard across her legs. The Hawken she leaned within easy reach. "There," she signed. "I am all set. Enjoy your rest."

The Crow studied her features before moving off. "I am old enough to be your father," he signed in parting, "but I tell you now that if I were twenty winters younger I would do my best to steal you away from Grizzly Killer."

Tiny fingers of flame were all that remained of the fire, casting a feeble glow. Bull Standing With Cow curled up next to it and pulled a blanket up over him.

It was the quiet time of the night, when the nocturnal predators were bedding down for the upcoming day and the daytime animals were not yet awake.

Winona rested her hands on her knees and listened to the whisper of the wind in the tall trees. Alone with her thoughts, she could not help but think of Nate. Was he still alive? Something deep within her assured her that he was, but that same something told her that he was in dire danger. She yearned to be with him.

Presently a few birds chirped, and it wasn't long afterward that the woods were filled with the avian chorus that always preceded the dawn.

Evelyn stirred but went back to sleep. Winona contented herself with holding her daughter close and shutting her mind to the apprehension gnawing at her insides.

A thin streak of pink appeared to the east. Winona turned her head to admire its brilliant hue and suddenly sensed that someone else was close by. Placing a hand on her pistol, she shifted.

He Dog had the look of an unkempt mongrel in a foul temper. He was unarmed, but his big fists were clenched as if to pound on anyone who dared antagonize him.

"Why do you stare at me?" Winona demanded. "What do you want?"

The warrior sneered at her. "What is wrong, woman? Do I make you uncomfortable? Does it fill you with fear? It should. Because before this is over with, you and that man of yours will regret treating me as you have." He nodded toward the plain. "Where is he, woman? Why is he taking so long? Is this a trick on your part to keep us from saving Fetches Water?"

The idea was so preposterous that Winona almost laughed. "Were you hit on the head by a falling tree?"

"Do not mock me," He Dog warned.

"Then do not say stupid things," Winona retorted. "Why would we want to stop you from rescuing her?"

"Your man is white, and whites are never to be trusted. They do not think like normal people, so who can say why they do what they do?"

"You talk in circles."

The warrior advanced but halted when she started to draw the flintlock. "Know this, woman. I intend to make Fetches Water my wife one day. Nothing will stop me from freeing her, not the Lakotas, not your husband, and certainly not you. If the mighty Grizzly Killer has not shown up by the time the sun is straight overhead, I am leaving to find her."

Winona watched him go off into the bushes. The day had gotten off to a wonderful start, and she feared that it would only get worse before it got better.

A lot worse.

* * *

David Thompson

A jostling motion revived Nathaniel King. That, and a knot of pain on the back of his head that throbbed insistently. His mouth felt as dry as a desert and his stomach was queasy. He became aware that he was lying on his stomach and that his wrists and ankles were bound.

Nate opened his eyes. He had been thrown over a sorrel being led by the Lakota warrior skilled with a rope. Other warriors rode on both sides of him, one leading his stallion and the pinto. They were talking quietly among themselves, completely ignoring him.

Dawn was at hand. Nate figured the band had been riding most of the night. They were climbing a grass-covered hill, and when they came to the top, they reined up.

Below lay a wide river glistening greenish-blue in the morning light. Shimmering cottonwoods, drooping willows and sturdy oaks fringed both banks. To the west a smaller river merged with the wider waterway, their junction dotted by gravel bars and tiny isolated islands of vegetation. To the east, the pristine main river wound off across the prairie until lost in the golden haze.

Nate knew where he was. The wide river was the Platte, the smaller river the South Platte. Which meant that the enormous village spread out between the two rivers had to be the encampment of the Oglala Lakotas.

Hundreds of lodges were arranged in traditional fashion, all with their entrances facing eastward. From many wafted tendrils of smoke. Dozens of women chatted at the rivers while filling water skins. A number of children and dogs were abroad. It was an idyllic setting, deceptively so since Nate knew the type of reception he would receive.

Two members of the returning band fired off rifles or fusees while others shouted and screeched.

Tepee flaps were thrown wide and people poured out to greet the newcomers. The women hurried from the rivers while the children ran to the edge of the camp.

Nate had witnessed the same event many times in Shoshone villages. Whenever warriors returned in triumph, they liked to make a grand entrance. It was customary if they arrived late at night to wait until the next day to ride in.

The returning Sioux formed into a long column with Nate at the center. Several had noticed he was awake, but they left him alone. He tried moving his arms and legs and soon gave it up as a lost cause.

Amid much fanfare, the warriors descended. Onlookers pressed forward for a glimpse of Nate. The men were openly hostile, the women were filled with glee, while many of the children made bold to dash up to him and tug at his hair or his clothes. Dogs sniffed and growled.

The Lakotas were much like Nate's adopted people, the Shoshones, in that they lived in buffalo hide lodges, and in the same style of dress. The men favored moccasins, breechcloths and buckskin leggings; the women were partial to leather dresses with short sleeves. Many had donned heavy buffalo robes to ward off the morning chill.

Generally speaking, the Lakotas were slightly smaller in stature than the Shoshones but much more muscular. They were a handsome people, and they carried themselves with dignity and pride.

The band headed for a particularly large lodge.

From within came a warrior who had more wrinkles than the prairie had blades of grass. His hair was streaked with gray and he walked with the aid of a long stick. Joining him were several middle-aged warriors, one sporting an elaborate headdress that hung almost down to the ground.

The warrior who had roped Nate in the gully now slid off his horse. Taking hold of Nate's arms, he pulled hard, dumping Nate at his feet. Nate instantly lashed out with both legs, striking the warrior in the shins. The man staggered but kept his footing and began to draw a knife. Only a stern word from the aged Lakota stopped him.

Two other warriors roughly hauled Nate upright. Another loosened the loops around his ankles so he could walk. He was shoved forward and tripped, landing on his knees in front of the tribal leaders.

A groan behind him was the first inkling Nate had that he wasn't the only captive. Gruff words were uttered. The next second Emmet Carter was pushed to the ground beside him.

The greenhorn was in bad shape. His entire right side was caked with dry blood from the arrow wound in his arm. The arm itself was badly swollen. His face bore bruises and welts and there was a nasty gash on his left temple. Bent at the waist, his eyes shut tight, he pressed the stiff limb against his stomach and moaned loudly.

Nate's feelings about the man had not changed one bit, but he felt compelled to nudge Emmet's elbow and say out of the corner of his mouth, "Quit bellyaching, Carter. You can't show any weakness. The Lakotas respect courage, not cowardice."

The younger man looked up. "King!" he exclaimed in amazement. "Am I glad to see you! I thought that these sons of bitches had lifted your scalp!"

"They could have at any time," Nate mentioned. "Which makes me suspect that they must have real special plans for us."

"What do we do? How do we get out of here?"

Before Nate could reply, the man in the war bonnet took two steps and kicked the greenhorn in the sternum. Carter was knocked onto his side and cried out shrilly. He made a feeble effort to stand, but cringed when the warrior drew back a leg to kick him again.

Some of the onlookers laughed.

"Don't just lie there!" Nate whispered. "Show them you have some gumption. Get up!"

"And be kicked again?" Carter said. "No thank you. I'll just stay out of their way until they lose interest in me."

"*That will never happen*," Nate stated, and was suddenly clipped on the shoulder by the warrior with the rope. He rocked with the blow but stayed on his knees.

A discussion broke out. The Lakota tongue was totally alien to Nate, so the best he could make out was that the older warriors were questioning the members of the war party about the greenhorn's capture, and his. The pair who had tried to pull him from the stallion spoke at length, as did the warrior with the rope. Finally the tall warrior who had put a shaft into Carter stepped forward and addressed the throng.

Nate didn't like the way the Sioux were staring at Emmet. Carter had doubled over with his forehead on the dirt and consequently didn't notice.

The ancient warrior was the last to speak. Whatever he said was short and to the point. He motioned once at Nate, once at Carter.

At a yell from the man in the headdress, the Lakotas converged. Iron hands gripped Nate and he was half carried, half dragged to a nearby lodge. Without ceremony he was tossed inside, smacking onto his shoulder and jarring his chin. Shrugging off the effects, Nate wriggled to the entrance and poked his head out the flap just as a terror-stricken scream wafted through the village.

A space had been cleared to the west of the big lodge and was ringed by Oglalas. A couple of warriors were dragging Emmet Carter toward a thick pole that had been hastily imbedded in the earth. He shrieked and kicked and thrashed, to no avail. Within moments he had been lashed to the pole and stripped buck naked.

Nate wanted to tear his eyes from the spectacle, but he could not. "I tried to warn him," he said softly to himself.

The warrior Carter had shot stepped through the crowd. He had been bandaged and carried his lance in his left hand. Trailing him was a chestnut which he mounted and rode to a point directly opposite Carter. Leveling the lance, he tucked it to his side.

Carter had stopped struggling and gawked at the Lakota in wide-eyed horror. When the Sioux started toward him, he turned beet-red in the face, then strained against the ropes in a frenzy, blubbering like a madman the whole while.

The Lakota picked up speed, gradually bringing the chestnut to a trot. As he neared the pole he leaned forward and extended the lance.

Emmet Carter was practically beside himself. "*Nooooo!*" he wailed. "No! No! No!"

The Sioux were holding their collective breath in tense anticipation. The only sounds other than the greenhorn's bawling cries were the rhythmic

GET
4 FREE BOOKS!

You can have the best Westerns delivered to your door for less than what you'd pay in a bookstore or online. Sign up for one of our book clubs today, and we'll send you 4 FREE* BOOKS, worth $23.96, just for trying it out...with no obligation to buy, ever!

Authors include classic writers such as
LOUIS L'AMOUR, MAX BRAND, ZANE GREY
and more; PLUS new authors such as
COTTON SMITH, TIM CHAMPLIN, JOHNNY D. BOGGS
and others.

As a book club member you also receive the following special benefits:
- 30% OFF all orders through our website & telecenter!
- Exclusive access to special discounts!
- Convenient home delivery and 10 days to return any books you don't want to keep.

There is no minimum number of books to buy,
and you may cancel membership at any time.
See back to sign up!

*Please include $2.00 for shipping and handling.

YES! ☐

Sign me up for the Leisure Western Book Club
and send my FOUR FREE BOOKS! If I choose to stay
in the club, I will pay only $14.00* each month,
a savings of $9.96!

NAME: _____

ADDRESS: _____

_____

TELEPHONE: _____

E-MAIL: _____

☐ **I WANT TO PAY BY CREDIT CARD.**

☐ VISA   ☐ MasterCard   ☐ DISCOVER

ACCOUNT #: _____

EXPIRATION DATE: _____

SIGNATURE: _____

Send this card along with $2.00 shipping & handling to:

**Leisure Western Book Club
20 Academy Street
Norwalk, CT 06850-4032**

Or fax (must include credit card information!) to: 610.995.9274.
You can also sign up online at www.dorchesterpub.com.

JOIN NOW!

pounding of the horse's flying hooves. They grew louder and louder as the horse went faster and faster and were punctuated by an ear-splitting screech of mortal anguish.

The lance sheared into Emmet Carter at the exact spot where his lead ball had penetrated the warrior, the point bursting out his back. The warrior let go and rode on around the pole to the acclaim of the onlookers.

Carter stiffened, then fainted. He hung as limp as a wet sack.

Kneeing the chestnut in front of the captive, the Lakota bent and wrenched the lance out. Blood and gore spewed forth with it. A brief lull ensued as he rode back into the crowd and climbed down.

Nate rested his cheek on the ground. His turn would be next, he was sure. He hoped that he would bear up better than Carter was doing. If, by some fluke, his family heard of his passing, he wanted them to be proud of him.

A commotion signaled the arrival of a half-dozen bowmen, among them the tall warrior and several others who had been at White Bark Creek. A woman bearing a hollow gourd walked out to Carter and splashed water on his face to revive him.

Carter took one look at the archers and went into hysterics. Disgust was evident on the faces of many of the Lakotas.

First to notch a shaft was the tall Sioux. He took deliberate aim.

Carter struggled mightily, swinging from side to side and shaking from head to toe in a futile bid to spoil the Lakota's aim.

With an audible twang the arrow streaked from the bow. The warrior had intentionally aimed low, and the arrow imbedded itself in the pole between

Carter's legs. Carter squealed like a stuck pig while the throng expressed their admiration of the warrior's skill.

The next warrior also missed. Likewise the third and the fourth. Each shaft, though, came a little closer to the figure at the pole than the shaft before it.

Then it was the tall man's turn again. Everyone, Carter included, knew that this time the warrior wouldn't miss. Carter repeated his insanely frantic jig. He hollered and begged and cried.

The arrow impaled him in the groin.

Nate wished he could cover his ears so he would not have to hear Emmet's pathetic high-pitched blubbering and whimpering. The man went on and on, quaking and weeping until even the Lakotas seemed to tire of hearing it and a second shaft imbedded itself in his left thigh. Another ripped into his right.

Carter raised his tear-streaked face to the blue sky and beseeched, "*Save me*! Dear Lord, please don't let this happen!"

Nate would have given anything to have a rifle. He crawled back into the lodge and lay curled into a ball in the gloomy interior. The thunk-thunk-thunk of arrows striking home sounded like the steady beat of a small drum. In due course Carter's blubbering dwindled to sorrowful sobs and occasional screams.

When next Nate peered out, Emmet Carter bristled with arrows yet somehow still lived. His head had not been touched and he turned it repeatedly as if seeking someone.

Abruptly, Carter trembled violently. "Forgive me my sins!" he croaked at the heavens. "I never meant—"

The next moment, he died.

Nate King rose onto his knees. Four Lakotas cut the body down. Each and every arrow was removed before the corpse was toted off to be left out on the prairie for scavengers to feast on.

Ground-hitched near the large lodge were the black stallion and Zach's paint. Nate gauged the distance, saw that none of the Oglalas were facing in that direction, and made a bid for freedom. Scooting out under the flap, he ran for all he was worth. He heaved against his bounds, but they were too tight.

Nate was astounded when he reached the horses without an outcry being raised. He darted to the off-side of the stallion and hiked his leg to slip his foot into the stirrup. By giving a little hop, he succeeded.

Now came the hard part. Nate coiled his left leg and jumped straight up, but he couldn't rise high enough to straddle the saddle. He had to stick his foot back in the stirrup before trying it again. The result was the same.

Frustrated, Nate ducked under the stallion and straightened next to the pinto. This time he might have better luck. It was much smaller.

In another two seconds Nate was mounted. Bending low, he pumped his legs. The horse slowly turned and he guided it toward the far side of the large lodge.

That was when shouts broke out.

Nate slapped his legs harder. The pinto began to pick up speed, but not nearly quick enough to suit him. He heard onrushing footsteps and swiveled just as a couple of fleet Lakotas leaped. With his hands bound he was helpless to prevent them from yanking him off the horse and throwing him bodily to the earth. He kicked and connected, but then more men arrived. His arms were clamped tight and he was jerked to his feet.

Over a score of warriors surrounded the trapper. Angry as riled hornets, they propelled him westward, retracing their steps past the lodge and hustling him toward the center of the ring of Lakotas.

And toward the pole drenched with Emmet Carter's blood.

Chapter Nine

He Dog did not wait until the sun was straight up. The golden orb was barely an hour high in the sky when he stood up and signed, "Enough of this waiting! I am going to find Fetches Water now. Anyone who wants, come with me."

Runs Against and Yellow Owl promptly rose and indicated they would join him. Two Humps objected verbally, and the next thing, all the Crows were embroiled in a vehement dispute in their own tongue.

Winona and Zach could do nothing except sit there and wait for the Crows to finish. The Hawken lay on a blanket at the Shoshone woman's side, and she picked it up and held it in her lap.

Soon all the warriors were on their feet, some gesturing angrily. Bull Standing With Cow was making an earnest appeal to He Dog, but judging by He Dog's expression he was wasting his time.

Winona was prepared when the stocky hothead,

Yellow Owl, Runs Against and Bear Ears headed for the horse string. Springing to her feet, she leveled the Hawken and cocked it.

At the metallic rasp, the four Crows halted. He Dog glared, then signed, "Do not try to stop us, woman."

Stepping a few paces to the left so her daughter would be out of the line of fire, Winona stood tall and said to Zach, "Translate for me. I dare not take my hands off the rifle."

"Sure, Ma," the boy responded. He had leaped up when his mother did, resolved to do whatever was necessary to protect her.

"Tell them this," Winona said, and her son began to relay her words as best sign language allowed. "Say that we agreed to help them because Two Humps is Grizzly Killer's friend. Say that we knew the dangers, but that did not stop us. We have risked all on their behalf, yet now we find that they have no respect for us and no regard for our lives."

"Your tongue speaks false," He Dog replied. "I am the only one who has a grudge against you. These others are leaving with me because they know I am right."

"Are you?" Winona rejoined. "Or are you letting your affection for Fetches Water cloud your mind?" She paused. "If you ride off, all our hard work in slipping into Lakota country undetected will have been for nothing. In broad daylight you are bound to be spotted sooner or later. The Oglalas will overwhelm you, and what will happen to Fetches Water then?"

"What do you think might be happening to her *now*?" He Dog said. "I am not going to waste more time when even as we speak a Lakota bastard might be forcing himself on her."

Winona lowered the muzzle a bit. So there it was. The real reason the warrior was so passionately determined to rescue the girl.

"If you intend to shoot, shoot," He Dog went on. "It will prove that you lie when you claim to be a friend of the Absarokas." He addressed the men with him, then added, "None of us will lift a finger against you. So squeeze the trigger." Holding his arms out, he faced her. "Shoot me if you really believe it is in Fetches Water's best interests."

Winona could not bring herself to do it.

He Dog nodded. "I did not think you had it in you to kill someone who is not trying to kill you, and I was right." He lowered his arms. "You need not go with us, woman. Stay and wait for your precious white man. By the time he shows up, we will have rescued Fetches Water."

"Ma?" Zach said as the four warriors stepped to their mounts. He raised his rifle, but his mother shook her head and eased down the hammer of her own. "Why are we just letting them ride off?"

What should she say? Winona mused. That in his twisted way, He Dog had a point about the greater danger to Fetches Water? That she could not bring herself to shoot him or any of the others down in cold blood? That she could not blame the Crows for not wanting to wait there forever for Nate?

"Ma?" Zach repeated.

Bull Standing With Cow approached. "I am sorry, my friends," he signed, "but we cannot let them go off by themselves. Two Humps, Flying Hawk and I must go along."

"I understand," Winona signed.

"I wish I did," Zach muttered aloud.

Winona stepped to her blanket and knelt to fold it. "Saddle our horses quickly, Stalking Coyote," she said. "We must go with them, too."

"But Pa told us to sit tight."

"He will find us eventually." Winona noticed Zach's confusion and elaborated by saying, "Think, son. What is one of the first things the Lakotas will do if they come on a band of Crows in their own country?"

"Attack them."

"Besides that."

"I don't—" Zach began, and abruptly recollected the time the Shoshones had found evidence of a Piegan band near their village. "Some of them will go after the Crows while others will backtrack to see if the band is part of a larger war party."

"And if the Sioux backtrack, where will that lead them?"

Zachary King looked at the tall trees and the bubbling creek and the stump. "Right here."

Nate King offered no resistance as the Lakotas pushed and shoved him over to the bloody pole. Outnumbered as he was, it would have been pointless. Plus, he wasn't about to do anything that smacked of rank cowardice. He would show them that not all white men were like Emmet Carter.

Hide thongs were used to bind the big trapper's hands and feet. One of the Sioux wore his beaver hat. His pistols had been claimed by two others. A fourth sported his knife in a beaded sheath. Wearing mocking grins, the warriors completed their task and walked back to where the bowmen were notching arrows to their strings.

Nate squared his shoulders and regarded the archers with forced detachment. The onlookers had fallen silent again. Among them was the ancient warrior, who studied Nate closely.

The tall warrior slowly elevated his bow. As he had done with Carter, he sighted carefully down the shaft. He aimed high, though, not low, and held himself perfectly still.

To Nate, it seemed as if the razor sharp tip were pointed straight at his heart. An urge to close his eyes came over him but he resisted it. His mouth felt dry, his palms damp. Suddenly the shaft flashed from the bow. He could see it clearly, see the glistening tip and the revolving feathers almost as if the arrow were moving in slow motion. For a heart-stopping moment he had the impression it was going to transfix his chest. Then there was a loud thud and the quivering shaft was so close to his neck that he could feel the smooth wood brushing his skin.

Nate's breath had caught in his throat. He let it out and willed himself to relax to calm the blood racing madly in his veins. His legs tingled as if from lack of blood and grew so weak that he had to exert all his willpower in order not to sag.

Another warrior moved forward to shoot. This one did not take nearly as long aiming. His string twanged and the arrow sped across the intervening space to sink into the pole on the other side of the trapper's neck.

Again Nate betrayed no fear. Some of the bowmen exchanged glances. Three more times arrows were shot, one sticking into the pole between his legs, two others missing his ears by the width of a hair.

The ancient warrior said something that caused the bowmen to lower their weapons. The tall one handed his to another man. Drawing a knife, the tall Lakota briskly advanced. When he was within five paces of the pole he gripped the knife by the blade and held it above his shoulder, poised to throw.

Nate locked his eyes on the Oglala's. No enmity was apparent. The warrior was simply doing what had to be done. He made his face muscles go rigid to keep from flinching. The very next instant the Lakota's arm whipped down and the knife leaped from his fingers.

The blade bit into the pole above Nate's head. He nearly grimaced when it nicked him. A moist sensation spread across his scalp and down past his left ear. He was bleeding.

Murmuring broke out among the assembled Sioux. The aged chief consulted with a handful of other apparent tribal leaders. Listening in were the tall warrior and the man who had snared Nate in the gully. The latter did not act pleased by whatever decision was reached. He protested vigorously. The gray-haired Lakota responded, and the roper walked off in a huff.

Nate was perplexed. He had expected to be accorded a swift and painless death if he demonstrated he was not afraid, but the Oglalas quite clearly had something else in mind. Several of them untied him from the pole, bound his wrists, and escorted him to the same small lodge in which he had initially been tossed. This time they did not treat him roughly. They even let him stoop and enter under his own power, perhaps out of respect.

Since the smoke flap at the top of the lodge was closed, Nate had to sit in near darkness and ponder what his next move should be.

That the Sioux had spared him was amazing. By all accounts they were not fond of whites and had already slaughtered a few trappers foolhardy enough to cross their territory.

Trail's End

Shakespeare McNair had once told Nate that many years ago the Lakotas and the whites had been on friendly terms. In fact, it had been an Englishman who first encountered them back when they lived along the Missouri River. On seeing that they used knives made of bone and stone, he had gone east and later returned with steel knives which he had handed out for free. Among the Minniconjou, among whom McNair had stayed for a short time over 40 years ago, that winter was known as They First Saw Steel Knives.

But sometime after that a dispute had arisen between several trappers and their Hunkpapa hosts. According to Shakespeare, the trappers had been drunk and one of them had stupidly insisted on making advances at the wife of a Hunkpapa leader.

None of the trappers had left the village alive. Ever since, there had been bad blood between the Lakotas and the whites.

So Nate had no reason to count on his reprieve being permanent. He figured that in their own sweet time the Oglalas would get around to finishing him off. They probably had something special planned for him, he mused, like the time he had been captured by Blackfeet and they had made him run a gauntlet.

Nate had to escape while he could. He decided to await nightfall and try. Moving over to the side of the lodge, he leaned against the buffalo hide to rest.

It could not have been more than a minute later that the flap was thrown wide and sunlight bathed him. He squinted as into the lodge came the tall warrior and the ancient leader. Straightening, he scrutinized their features for a clue as to why they were there, but both men were inscrutable.

The older man knelt and set his staff down. At a nod from him, the tall warrior cut Nate loose. The chief's gnarled hands moved slowly as he resorted to sign language, saying, in essence, "I am called Ant. I was born Minniconjou but came to live with the Oglalas when I took an Oglala woman as my mate."

Nate signed, "I am Grizzly Killer, a Shoshone."

Ant's features crinkled in wry humor. "How strange. You do not look like any Snake I have ever known. Or do the Shoshones now dress and act like white men?"

"They took me into their tribe when I took one of their women as *my* mate."

The leader chuckled. "It does not surprise me to learn this. The Snakes know a brave man when they see one." Ant gazed at the lodge wall as if peering into his own past. "I have lived longer than any Lakota alive, so I have counted many coup, fought many enemies. And none have ever shown more courage than the Snakes." He paused. "The Absarokas are brave, too, but they do not like to do battle unless they stand a good chance of winning. The Hohe would rather flee than fight. As for the Flatheads, they resist when they are attacked, but once they start to lose, they run. Practice has made them good runners, too. I never could catch one."

Nate did not know what to make of the old warrior's friendliness, so he made no comment.

"Question. What was the name of your friend who did not die so well?" Ant inquired.

"He was not my friend," Nate signed. "I was hunting him down to kill him when the man beside you found us."

Ant and the tall warrior conversed briefly. "Were those your shots Thunder Hoop and the rest of the war party heard?"

"The white man was firing at me," Nate detailed. "He had stolen a horse and two guns from my family and he knew I wanted them back." He also remarked, "As for his name, it can only be said in the white tongue." Aloud, Nate stated, "Emmet Carter."

Ant tried to say it several times but could not accent the syllables properly. "It twists the tongue," he conceded. "So from now on we will refer to him as He Who Bawled."

Thunder Hoop had not resheathed his knife. He did place it on his leg to sign, "Tell us, Grizzly Killer, why were you in our country?"

"I was chasing He Who Bawled," Nate reiterated. "He did not know this was land the Oglala roamed."

"He did not know much at all, if you ask me," Ant said. "Who taught him how to be a man?" The warrior made a clucking noise. "Such weaklings reflect poorly on a people."

"I could not agree more."

Ant clasped his hands and was quiet for a short spell. "What are we to do with you, Grizzly Killer? Many want to kill you and be done with you, but there is a quality about you I like. There is something I see in your eyes that tells me you are a man much like myself."

"You flatter me."

"You also remind me of the first white man I knew. We called him The Knife Bringer. He gave the Minnniconjou many steel knives when I was barely old enough to walk. I can still remember my father holding his close to the fire every night to admire the fine steel."

So the story Shakespeare had told Nate was true. He made bold to sign, "Not all white men are bad. Even though your warrior captured me and brought me here against my will, I bear the Oglalas no ill will. Nothing would please me more than to be able to smoke the pipe of peace with you and call you my brother."

Ant acted pleased. "I would be just as honored. But that cannot be, for you have admitted that you are a Snake now, not a white man, and the Snakes are our enemies." His fingers hung in the air a moment. "We kill our enemies."

Nate had tried. He did not let his disappointment show.

"Or most of our enemies," Ant amended his statement. "We do not make war on women and children, as the Blackfeet and Absarokas do. I still remember the time three women went off to cut wood and the Crows rubbed them out."

Nate took a gamble. "Is it true that your people raided the Absarokas within the past couple of moons?"

"Yes," Ant signed proudly. "Our warriors slew many Crows and stole many horses. They also brought back captives who will be reared as Oglalas. In time they will forget they were ever anything else." He indicated the tall warrior. "Thunder Hoop was on that raid. He counted four coup. And he brought back a pretty girl who will soon be married off to a deserving man."

"Is her Crow name Fetches Water?"

Ant was surprised. "It is. How did you know, Grizzly Killer?"

"A friend of mine heard about the raid from a Crow who was there," Nate hedged.

Thunder Hoop wasn't satisfied. "Since when do Absarokas get along well with Snakes?" he asked suspiciously.

"I did not say my friend was a Shoshone," Nate

responded. "Remember I was born white, and the whites get along well with both tribes."

The tall warrior and the aged leader talked at length. Ant signified the parley was at an end by picking up his stick and pushing off the ground. "It has been a pleasure meeting you, Snake Who Is White. Tonight we hold a council to see what we will do with you. I, for one, will propose that we grant you a death due a true warrior."

"I thank you," Nate replied sincerely, and did not object when Thunder Hoop tied his wrists behind his back.

The moment the flap closed behind them, Nate scooted to it and peeked under the bottom edge. Ant walked off toward the big lodge while the tall warrior entered a tepee further away. Painted on its side was a lightning bolt in the shape of a circle.

The horses were back in front of the council lodge. Both had been hobbled.

Nate would have liked to note more details, but a pair of moccasins materialized before his eyes.

The Sioux had posted a guard.

"This is a mistake, Ma," Zachary King declared. "I can feel it in my bones."

Winona shared her son's sentiments, but she goaded her mare northward anyway. They had gotten ready to go as swiftly as they could, yet they were well behind the two groups of Crows.

He Dog and his three companions had ridden out first, deliberately leaving everyone else behind, and were now a quarter of a mile ahead of Two Humps, Bull Standing With Cow, and Flying Hawk, who in turn were well ahead of the Shoshone and her son.

"Doesn't He Dog have any brains at all? Doesn't

he see that being strung out like this is asking for trouble?" Zach groused.

"I doubt he cares."

"He doesn't care whether he lives or dies?"

Several dark shapes had appeared on the horizon to the west. Winona was studying them to insure they were buffalo and not Lakotas. "He Dog is in love with Fetches Water. All he cares about is saving her."

Zach rose and shielded his eyes from the glare so he could see the four warriors who were in the lead. "It's awful hard for me to imagine a man like him caring for anybody."

"Love can be a mystery at times," Winona agreed. "But never doubt its power, son. It is stronger than the muscles of the mightiest man, more lasting than the sky above and the earth below. Love is forever."

The youth mulled that over for the next five miles.

On all sides the high grass rustled in the breeze. Coyotes slunk off at their approach, and on two occasions antelope gave flight in great bounding leaps. Scattered clusters of buffalo regarded the riders with the patent belligerence of their shaggy breed.

Winona hardly noticed the wildlife. All she cared about was spotting Oglalas before any Oglalas spotted them. Blue Flower was awake and uttered soft sounds every now and then. Shortly before midday Winona slowed, shrugged out of the cradleboard, and breast-fed her daughter on horseback.

Zach was on proverbial pins and needles. It was dreadful, being exposed out in the open in the middle of hostile territory. His worry was more for his mother and sister than for himself. He couldn't abide the notion of either of them coming to harm.

He Dog and his three friends never slowed, not even at noon as had been the war party's habit. They pushed on north toward the junctions of the South Platte and the Platte.

The afternoon waxed and began to wane. Winona was thankful for the absence of Lakotas, but she was also mystified. They were so near traditional Oglala haunts that it defied belief they had not encountered any Sioux yet.

At one point Zach shifted to scan the flat ocean of prairie to their rear. He observed how the grass had a knack for springing back up after the horses went by, and it provoked a question. "Are you sure Pa will be able to track us? I know I'd have a hard time."

"Your father was taught by one of the best trackers alive, Shakespeare McNair. He will find us," Winona avowed, while inwardly she suppressed a latent fear that he might not.

Zach felt like talking to take his mind off his worries, so he mentioned, "I've always sort of liked the plains. But to be honest, Ma, I don't think I could ever live out here."

"Why not?" Winona prompted.

"Take a gander. It's too darned flat. And boring. What good does it do for a body to be able to see as far as the eye can see if there's not a blamed thing worth looking at?" Zach shook his head. "No, ma'am. Give me the high country, where there are peaks that nearly touch the clouds and snow pretty near all year long and a person never knows what is over the next ridge."

Up ahead, Two Humps had slowed. Winona saw him straighten and stare toward He Dog's bunch.

"Do you feel that way, too?" Zach asked.

Absently, Winona said, "Where I live is not so important to me. What is important is that I be with my man and my children. I could be happy anywhere if Nate were happy too."

"You do like our cabin, though, don't you? And where it is and all?"

Winona reined up. It was difficult for her to distinguish details, but there seemed to be a commotion among the foremost Crows. Her nerves jangled when she realized He Dog, Runs Against, Bear Ears and Yellow Owl were racing back toward Two Humps and company. "No!" she said softly.

"What is it?" Zach asked, following her gaze. He saw Two Humps. He saw He Dog. And he saw a large band of warriors bearing down on them. At that distance they were no more than a blur, but he didn't need to see them clearly to know who they were.

Lakotas.

Chapter Ten

Darkness seemed to take forever to descend. The afternoon dragged by as if every minute were weighted down by two-ton boulders.

Nate King did not waste a single one of them. Within moments after discovering a guard had been posted, he moved back into the deepest patch of shadow at the rear of the lodge and commenced striving his utmost to slip free of the thongs binding his wrists. He strained. He yanked and tugged. He worked his hands back and forth.

The pain became excruciating. At length Nate's muscles ached clear up to his shoulders. Worst of all was the agony in both wrists, compounded when the skin split, making them slick with blood.

Thunder Hoop had done his job well. Hours of effort hardly loosened the loops. Yet he refused to concede defeat. Teeth grit, perspiration beading his brow, blood dripping from his fingers, he rubbed and chafed and heaved without cease.

It was about an hour before sunset when low voices right outside the flap drew Nate to the entrance. A peek showed that another warrior was taking the place of the first man. They were talking and joking. In a little while the first man departed and his lean replacement stepped to the right of the flap and stood there with the butt of a slender lance propped at his feet.

Nate noted the lengths of the shadows of the nearest tepees, then crept back to the rear. He was running out of time. At the rate he was going, it would be morning before he freed himself, and his wrists would be in such bad shape it would be a miracle if he didn't bleed to death first.

Inspiration born of desperation came to him. Nate sat on his haunches and tucked his knees as tightly to his chest as he could. Then, exerting every ounce of strength his powerful frame possessed, he attempted to slide his hands down over his buttocks.

It appeared to be an impossible challenge. More precious minutes went by as Nate pushed and wriggled and hiked his backside off the ground again and again. Yet he barely moved his hands an inch and a half.

His sense of urgency mounting, Nate eased onto his left side and reapplied himself. He shimmied like a snake while hunching his posterior and extending his arms as far as he could. A fraction at a time his wrists dipped lower. He had to bow his elbows outward to get his forearms past his thighs, and even then it did not seem to be enough to do the trick.

Nate could never say what suddenly made him stop and glance at the entrance. Call it gut instinct. Call it a premonition. Whichever, as he looked up the flap parted and the head of the Oglala poked inside.

The warrior was still a few seconds as his eyes adjusted. Then he spied the trapper and nodded to himself that all was well. The flap closed behind him.

Nate took up where he had left off. He found that by repeatedly lifting his rump while simultaneously hunching his shoulders until they throbbed, he could work his wrists downward by partial degrees. Again and again and again he did it, his arms screaming at him to stop.

Then came the moment Nate had worked so hard toward, the exhilarating instant when his bloody hands worked loose and were under his legs. The strain on his arms evaporated. He took but a second to gird himself, then snaked his arms up and around his legs and feet.

Nate sat up. Wiping his hands on his pants, he bent and applied his teeth to the thongs. The salty taste of blood filled his mouth. He chewed as if he were starved and this were his last meal. The leather was tough but had been softened somewhat by the blood and all his tugging. Like an oversized beaver, he gnawed through loop after loop.

His joy was unbounded when his hands fell free. They ached abominably and he had to move his fingers a while to relieve the stiffness. When they were back to normal, he rose in a crouch and stalked to the flap.

Twilight claimed the Lakota encampment. It was a tranquil time of day, when families were gathered together to eat and few people were abroad. Even the dogs were inside, awaiting their nightly scraps. Smoke from scores of cooking fires wafted from as many lodges. Horses stood quietly or grazed on sweet grass.

The warrior standing guard had moved a few more steps to the right and was leaning on the lance. If his expression were any indication, he was bored half to death.

A few pebbles lay near the flap. Nate inched his hands out far enough to retrieve one. He checked to verify there were no Lakotas in the immediate area, then flicked the pebble high into the air, between the guard and the lodge. When it hit about ten feet away, the warrior idly gazed in that direction, seeking the cause.

Nate silently pushed the flap outward and uncoiled. Careful to stay close to the tepee, he placed each foot down silently. He was almost within arm's length of the Oglala when the man yawned and pivoted toward him.

It was hard to say which of them was more surprised. The Sioux opened his mouth to alert the camp but Nate stifled the shout with a quick jab to the chin that staggered the warrior. Stunned, the Lakota speared the lance tip at him. Nate parried the thrust with a forearm and delivered another punch, this one an uppercut that rocked the Sioux on his heels. The warrior's legs crumpled, and as he fell Nate connected a third time.

The Oglala was unconscious when he slumped prone. Swiftly Nate stooped, hooked his hands under the man's arms, and dragged the warrior inside before anyone could notice.

No outcries were raised. The village lay undisturbed under the darkening sky.

Nate hastily stripped the Lakota of his knife and lance. He cut strips from the warrior's leggings and used them to tie the man's limbs and fit a gag in place.

Time was growing short. It would not be long

before the headmen of the tribe converged on the big lodge for the council Ant had mentioned.

Nate emerged, then hesitated. The stallion and the pinto were 20 yards off. It would be child's play for him to escape. All he had to do was dash over to them, mount up, and slip into the darkness.

But he couldn't. Not yet.

Somewhere to the south a dog barked as Nate hurried toward the lodge bearing the painted emblem of the circular lightning bolt. Murmuring forewarned him that others besides the tall warrior were inside.

Crouching beside the closed flap, Nate lightly pried at the edge and parted it a crack. A fire crackled softly. Hovering over a buffalo paunch in which boiled the family's supper was a woman Thunder Hoop's age. The warrior himself sat toward the back of the lodge, facing the entrance. He was engaged in conversation with a man half his years, perhaps a son. Two younger women were over by the left wall, preparing food.

Fetches Water was also there. The different style of her long dress and her braided hair marked her as not being Lakota. Huddled next to a pile of folded robes, her pretty features downcast, the Crow avoided looking at her captors.

Nate backed off before he was spotted. How could he get her out of there without raising a ruckus? he asked himself.

To the west a flap opened and an older woman stepped out. She went off toward the Platte, a water skin in hand.

Rising, Nate strolled to his horses. It was a test of his nerves to walk along as if he didn't have a care in the world so that he would not arouse suspicion if seen from a distance. Darting behind

135

them, he drew the butcher knife and cut the hobbles on both animals.

The flap to the council lodge was open. Within glowed a small fire, and someone chanted in a singsong voice.

Nate snuck to the opening and risked a look. Ant sat crosslegged, his arms on his knees, his wrinkled face upraised, his eyes closed. Placing the lance down, Nate slipped inside and circled to the left, staying in shadows. The old warrior droned on.

To the southeast a horse whinnied. Voices sounded. Nate halted and listened, dreading that the Lakotas had found the bound warrior. But the voices were much too distant.

Ant abruptly stopped chanting and cocked his head as if he were listening also. When he had satisfied himself that all was well, he lifted his head and resumed.

Nate cat-footed up behind the ancient warrior. At the touch of his blade to the side of Ant's neck, the Lakota stiffened and fell silent. Nate warily moved to the right without relaxing the pressure so the chief could see him.

Ant's dark eyes sparkled with mirth. He actually smiled and spoke a few words in his tongue. Slowly lifting his arms, he signed, in so many words, "It is good to see you again, Snake Who Is White. But I did not think it would be so soon."

Lowering the blade, Nate wedged it under the front of his belt so it was within ready reach, and responded, "I do not desire to harm you. I do not want to hurt any of your people. With your help, I will not have to."

"How kind. I will be sure to tell all one hundred and twenty-nine warriors in our village when they surround you."

Nate stood and motioned for the Oglala to do the same. "Even the loss of one man is one too many. Whether anyone dies will be up to you."

"How can that be? I am not the one who has a weapon."

"You are the one whom your people look up to the most, the one they will listen to if things do not go as I have planned."

"And what would you have me tell them?" Ant asked as he reached for his staff.

"That is for you to decide."

Nate helped the aged warrior rise, then steered him to the opening. He left the lance where it was, took Ant's elbow, and walked toward Thunder Hoop's lodge.

Suddenly a large dog appeared and padded toward them. He slowed to sniff noisily and studied Nate as if he could not quite make up his mind whether Nate was supposed to be there or not.

Ant spoke sharply, waving the staff. The dog veered to the north and was soon gone. "That is Crow Rising's animal," he signed. "He lets it wander as it pleases. It is always sticking its nose where it does not belong." He sighed. "In the old days, someone would have carved it up long before this to teach Crow Rising a lesson."

Nate used sign to say, "When we get there, announce yourself. I will be behind you, so do not try anything. Only take four steps inside, no more."

"If I take five will you cut off my ears? I know that is what I would do if I were in your place. Chopping off an ear is always a good way to get another man's attention. It hurts, but it does not kill him."

It was hard for Nate to tell whether the Lakota was serious or not. As they neared the lodge he slid to the rear and drew the knife.

Ant gave the hide flap a whack. Thunder Hoop called out and Ant replied. At a single word from Thunder Hoop, Ant pushed the flap aside with his long stick, then bent to go in.

All the occupants had shifted toward the entrance. Nate made it a point to keep the chief between himself and the others until Ant had taken the required four steps. Then he showed himself, the blade resting against Ant's neck.

One of the women gasped. Another dropped the parfleche she had been rummaging in. The young man barked something and started to lunge toward a lance which had been propped against the wall. Thunder Hoop stopped him with a single word.

Nate knew that every second was critical. He jabbed a thumb at Fetches Water and beckoned. She gawked, not knowing what to make of him, and made no move to comply. Again Nate beckoned, yet she sat there like a proverbial bump on a log.

During the long ride from the remote Rockies, Nate had heard the other Crows call Bull Standing With Cow by his name many times. He repeated that name now and was rewarded by having the girl leap to her feet with a hand clutched to her throat. She repeated her father's name, her lilt framing a question. Once more Nate said it, smiling to show he was on her side. He smiled and nodded at the flap.

The young Crow had to have her doubts. A white man she had never met had burst into the lodge of Lakotas who were holding her against her will and acted as if he wanted to help her. So Nate didn't hold it against her when she moved with all the speed of a turtle toward the opening.

Thunder Hoop made no move to interfere. His eyes betrayed keen resentment, but he did not go for the knife at his side nor for the bow lying nearby. His hands on his legs, he watched with the eyes of a hawk, awaiting an opening he could exploit.

The warrior's son, though, was another matter. He couldn't sit still and kept glancing at the lance. Had his father not been there, he would have grabbed it and attacked.

Nate never took his eyes off the younger one. When Fetches Water went on by and he heard the flap move, he backed up, gently pulling the chief with him as a shield. At the entrance he put his free hand on the Lakota's shoulder and pressed. Ant got the idea. Together they backed on out and Nate threw the flap shut.

The young Crow was waiting, poised like a terrified fawn to bolt at the first threat.

Pointing at the horses, Nate hustled Ant toward them. He saw Thunder Hoop and the son look out of the lodge, but neither raised an alarm. They wouldn't, not so long as they feared that he would slay Ant.

Fetches Water went to climb on the stallion, but Nate snapped his fingers to get her attention and indicated the pinto. She was on its back in a twinkling, raring to go. Nate stepped to the stallion, gripped its mane, and vaulted up.

Ant stepped close so that only Nate could see his hands move. "Your bluff worked, Snake Who Is White. It does my heart good to know that there is one white man left who is not a weakling."

The girl's impatience was growing but Nate had to ask, "If you knew I was bluffing, why did you do as I wanted?"

"I am fond of my ears," Ant said, grinning as he

moved closer to his lodge.

Wheeling the stallion to the east, Nate brought it to a gallop. Fetches Water did not leave his side, her walnut-sized eyes casting to the right and the left as if she thought the very shadows would spring out at them.

They had covered ten feet when Thunder Hoop's bellow boomed loud and clear. More shouts ensued, and soon the cries were being spread on all sides as here and there Lakotas scrambled from their dwellings.

Nate had picked eastward because there were fewer tepees to pass before reaching the prairie. They rushed on by four of them without incident. Then, from the next, a warrior holding a bow spilled out. The man spotted them and tried to notch a shaft. Without missing a beat, Nate cut the stallion and slammed into the Lakota, sending him flying.

A rifle cracked. Maybe Nate's own Hawken. But the shooter was aiming at moving objects in the dark, and missed. Before another shot rang out or any arrows could be unleashed, they sped out onto the plain and were embraced by the inky veil of night.

Nate wasn't fooled. They had escaped from the village, but they were still in mortal danger. The uproar in their wake was all the proof needed that within a span of minutes every last warrior would be on their trail.

All 129 of them.

Miles to the south lay a dry wash littered with small stones and bits of wood and grass. Ages ago it had been a robust stream fed by runoff from a majestic mountain to the west. But a landslide on a barren slope had altered the course of the runoff forever, and in practically no time at all the stream had withered and dried up and was now home to isolated pockets of weeds and an occasional snake.

At that exact moment it also sheltered a Shoshone woman and her two children.

Winona King had spotted the wash shortly after turning and fleeing southward at sight of the Lakotas. It ran from west to east but turned to the north at the spot where she glimpsed its outline. Had it not been for a break in the high grass, she would never have noticed it at all.

Without hesitation, Winona had reined sharply and trotted down to the bottom. Its banks had proven high enough to hide the horses, so she had quickly traveled a stone's throw to the first bend and on around.Drawing rein, she had slid off, then ran as fast as she could with the heavy cradleboard on her back to the point where the horses had descended.

Zach was with her every step of the way. He divined her plan the moment he saw the wash and prayed the ruse would work.

Winona started to arrange the grass they had trampled so the wash would not be visible unless someone was right next to it. But the clatter of hooves gave her pause.

"What's wrong, Ma?" Zach asked.

"Two Humps and those with him. We must signal them so they can join us."

Zach didn't like the idea one bit. Since they had been the farthest south when He Dog blundered onto the Lakotas, it was entirely possible the Oglalas hadn't seen them. But the Sioux were bound to have noticed the second group of Crows. Attracting Two Humps to the wash might give their location away. "Are you sure that's a good idea?" he wondered.

"No, but we must do it," Winona said. The safe thing to do would be to let the three Crows go on by. And the other Crows, too. Then the Lakotas would sweep on past their sanctuary without a sideways glance. But that meant denying aid to friends who needed it.

The clatter grew louder. Winona rose high enough to see Two Humps, Bull Standing With Cow, and Flying Hawk. They were 60 or 70 yards to the north and almost the same distance to the east. Well beyond them were He Dog, Runs Against, Yellow Owl and Bear Ears. The latter was bent over, clinging to his mount's mane, apparently wounded.

Even farther back were the Lakotas, 15 all told, thirsting for Crow blood. Whooping and flourishing their weapons, they rode as if they and their animals were one.

Winona exposed her head and shoulders, then waved. Two Humps and those with him were so intent on outracing their pursuers that they were looking neither to the right nor the left. She pumped both arms, hollering in Shoshone, "Two Humps! Bull Standing With Cow! Over here!"

None of the three men looked in her direction, perhaps because Flying Hawk was lashing his horse with his quirt and yelling.

"Here! Look this way!" Winona cried in English, jumping so they would see her.

Against his better judgment, Zach did likewise, screeching at the top of his lungs. "Are the three of you hard of hearing? Stop!"

The trio of Crows were abreast of the wash but 50 yards out. Bull Standing With Cow stiffened as if he heard them, yet then he looked off in the opposite direction and did not slow down.

"No!" Winona railed. "Please! We're over here!"

"Here! Here!" Zach echoed.

Unheeding, the warriors flew onward, their horses raising a thick cloud of dust.

"They'll never spot us now!" Winona declared, and took several strides. She was too late. The dust obscured the warriors, just as it would prevent them from seeing her.

Zach felt sorry for their friends, but there was nothing else that could be done; He Dog and the others were rapidly approaching. It galvanized him into springing to his mother and clasping her wrist. "come on, Ma! Those Lakotas will spot you if we stand out here much longer!"

Her son was right. Winona could see the foremost Oglalas clearly. And while she was willing to risk her life and those of her offspring to help the first three Crows, she would not endanger her loved ones for the four whose own stubbornness had brought misfortune down on their heads.

Winona and Zach dashed into the wash and crouched at the rim. They spread the grass stems to hide their passage. No sooner were they done than He Dog and those with him fled madly on by. An arrow jutted from the back of Bear Ears, who swayed precariously.

In the time Zach could have counted to ten, the Lakotas were there. In a tight knot the fierce warriors flashed past, half of them no more than vague shadows in the dust. Zach had his rifle pressed to his shoulder, but the Lakotas had eyes only for the bitter enemies in front of them.

Winona watched the Oglalas until they were out of sight. A twinge of guilt assailed her for not even trying to save He Dog's group. After all, she mused, she'd be just as impetuous and reckless if it had been Grizzly Killer or Stalking Coyote or Blue Flower who had been taken captive.

She shrugged off the self-recriminations. No one could hold it against her for doing what had to be done. Crying over spilt milk, as her man liked to say, was a waste of time and energy.

Sitting, Winona removed the cradleboard to check on her daughter. Evelyn wore the patient angelic smile of the very innocent, and giggled when Winona held her tiny fingers and blew on them.

"Well, we did it," Zach commented in amazement. "We gave those buzzards the slip. But since we're all alone in the middle of their territory, with Pa nowhere to be found, I have a question for you."

Winona looked at him.

"What do we do now, Ma?"

Chapter Eleven

The Lakotas were known far and wide as formidable warriors. In later years they would be one of the last Plains tribes to submit to the U.S. government's relentless campaign of Indian subjugation. Only when their way of life, embodied in the buffalo, had been almost exterminated, and their women and children were starving, did the last proud remnants submit to government control.

But in the early decades of the 1800s, the Lakotas were still a proud and free people, lords of all they surveyed. In battle they held their own against the powerful Blackfoot Confederacy to their north and against the Crows and Snakes to the west.

All white men had heard of their prowess as fighters and trackers. Nate King among them. So he knew that his chances of eluding the scores of riders who fanned out from the Platte River encampment in dozens of small groups were next to nil. Still, he had to try. Circumstance and experience had forged him into a man who never gave up no matter how great the odds against him.

As Nate and Fetches Water looped to the south after having ridden for two miles due east, he mulled over the situation.

The darkness worked in their favor in that it hid them from the Oglalas. But it also could work against them by concealing a band of warriors until Nate and the girl were right on them.

The Sioux also had the advantage of knowing the region well, since they spent several moons there every summer and had been doing so for many years.

Nate stopped often to listen. So far the sounds of pursuit had been faint; occasional hoofbeats to the west and north, a few shouts to the southwest.

The big trapper held to a brisk walk for the next hour to reduce the noise they made. There was no moon but enough starlight to bathe the rippling grass in a pale glow. He ascertained direction by the North Star and other celestial constellations, a knack every seasoned mountaineer developed if he wanted to last long in the wilderness.

Fetches Water did not let out a peep. She stopped when he did, listened when he listened. His smiles served to bolster her confidence, but she was still a nervous wreck. Distant sounds made her stiffen and gasp.

Nate had an added worry in the form of his family. By this time, he reasoned, they were probably wondering what had happened to him. If they had followed his instructions, they should be about 30 to 40 miles south of the Platte. But if they hadn't, if the impatient Crows had pushed on, then they might be much closer. In which case there was a very real likelihood the Sioux might stumble on them while hunting for the girl and him.

The prairie was alive with other sounds besides those made by the Lakotas. Coyotes yipped. Wolves howled their plaintive refrains. Grizzlies growled and painters screamed.

Nighttime was "the killing time," as a trapper Nate knew had once put it. The hours of darkness brought countless savage predators out of their dens to roam in search of hapless prey. Meat eaters preferred the mantle of inky gloom to the blazing brightness of the sun. At night they could prowl undetected, and pounce when least expected.

Nate tensed when a snort and a guttural cough pinpointed a bear less than a hundred feet to the northeast. He knew that it might be a harmless black bear, but he wasn't about to take anything for granted.

They angled to the southwest for a mile or so. The cough wasn't repeated, so Nate figured they had given the beast the slip.

Gradually the stars overhead changed position as the hours went by. It was the middle of the night when Nate felt safe in stopping briefly to rest the horses. Dismounting, he let the stallion graze while he walked off a few yards to survey the benighted prairie.

The Crow girl joined him. She didn't like to be left alone and it showed. Nervously rubbing her palms together, she stared bleakly toward the Platte.

"Do not worry," Nate signed. "They will not find us. Soon you will be back with your father."

The knowledge of sign language was not a skill restricted to men. So the girl was quick to respond, "Who are you, white man, that you help

147

me this way? How do you know of my father?"

Nate signed, "I am Grizzly Killer, a friend of Two Humps. I was once brought to your village as a prisoner of the Invincible One, but I later showed your people that he was not all he claimed to be."

"I remember you now," the girl said. "My father always said that your medicine is more powerful than anyone he ever met."

Over the next few minutes Nate explained how Bull Standing With Cow had asked for his help. He did not reveal Carter's treachery, nor did he see fit to mention his scrape with He Dog, although he did tell her the names of the warriors who had accompanied her father.

"So He Dog is with you," Fetches Water said somberly. "I should have known he would come."

"You do not seem happy about it."

The girl frowned. "Soon I will be old enough to take a husband. He Dog wants me, and he has let it be known that anyone else who courts me will answer to him. I am afraid he will be my only suitor."

Nate sympathized. Coming of age was a special event in the life of an Indian girl. It was usually marked by an elaborate ceremony. Then, depending on her attractiveness and popularity, she would be courted by as many men who were interested.

The courtship was strictly chaperoned. Potential suitors would show up in front of the family's lodge with a buffalo robe over their shoulders. If the girl was so inclined, she would take turns slipping under the robes of those lucky enough to catch her eye and spend time whispering and perhaps fondling one another. She could refuse to be embraced, and she was always free to slip out from under the robe whenever she so desired.

In time one of her suitors might make bold to send a friend to her father's lodge with however many horses the suitor could spare. If the girl accepted his marriage proposal, she took the horses to water or added them to her father's herd. If she wasn't interested, she sent the horses back or paid no attention to them.

There were few hurt feelings. In most instances the young men knew if their sweethearts would accept or not. At other times, the unions were arranged in advance by the parents of both parties.

For He Dog to assert that Fetches Water was going to be his, no matter what, was a serious breach of tribal etiquette. If he were allowed to carry through with his threat, it would ruin one of the grandest phases of the young girl's life.

"Any young man who truly cares for you will not let He Dog scare him off," Nate consoled her. "I would guess that you end up having more suitors than you know what to do with."

"I hope so."

They listened but heard no riders. Nate was eager to go on, so they were under way within a short while. Their little talk, he observed, had served to ease some of the girl's anxiety; she did not ride as stiffly as before.

About four in the morning, just when Nate was beginning to think that they actually had a prayer of getting away, the wind wafted low voices to them from the west. Stopping, he put a finger to his lips to caution the girl not to speak.

The sound faded, but Nate made no move to go on. Soon the wind picked up again, and with it came the indistinct words of whoever was out there. The language being used was hard to identify, but Nate suspected it was the tongue of the Oglalas.

Slipping off the stallion, Nate gestured for the girl to stay where she was, then he drew his knife and stalked off to investigate. He could move rapidly thanks to the wind, which rustled the grass so loudly that his movements would go unnoticed.

Unexpectedly Nate came on a shallow basin he estimated to be a hundred feet across. Huddled beside a tiny fire at the bottom were five Lakotas. Their horses were lined up behind them.

It was one of the search parties. The men were tired and had elected to rest until daylight. A few were munching on pemmican, and at the sight of it Nate's rumbling stomach nearly gave him away. He backed up a few feet so they wouldn't hear and suddenly bumped into something that had not been there a minute ago.

Thinking that the Oglalas had posted sentries and he had bumped into one, Nate whirled, bringing the knife up for a thrust. He checked his swing almost too late, then grabbed Fetches Water by the arm and drew her into the grass where he signed, "I told you to stay with the horse. Do you realize that I nearly stabbed you?"

"I refuse to be by myself," the girl responded, "so I tied them and followed you."

She was young but she was resolute. Nate knew he'd be wasting his breath if he tried to convince her to go back and wait for him. So, easing onto his elbows, he snaked to the basin with her at his side.

Three of the warriors the trapper recognized. One was the man who had staked a claim to his fine beaver hat. Another had a flintlock and Nate's powder horn and ammo bag. Still another was the Sioux so adept at roping.

Nate would have given anything to get his effects back, especially the pistol. Without a gun he felt half naked. He might as well wish on a star, though, since it would be certain suicide for him to charge on down there and seek to overpower five armed warriors.

Or would it?

Grasping the girl's hand, Nate led her to their mounts. By sign, he conveyed his intentions.

Fetches Water regarded him as if he were insane. "Do not do this thing, Grizzly Killer. You will only get yourself slain. Some food and a gun are not worth your life."

"I also want my hat back," Nate reminded her as he stepped to the stallion. Winking, he swung up. "If something happens, head due south. In less than two sleeps you will come to a creek. Your father and the Crow war party should be there."

"Please," the girl signed.

Bending, Nate patted her head as he went by. He clucked to the stallion and swung wide to the north to approach the basin from a different direction. That way, if he was rubbed out and the Lakotas backtracked him at first light, the girl would have ample time to get away.

Holding the knife at his waist, Nate flattened on the big stallion's broad back. At a plodding walk he neared the west rim. With the black sky in the background, he felt confident the warriors wouldn't spot him.

When the Lakotas materialized, Nate stopped. Their five horses were directly below him. He smiled to himself as he slowly straightened, tossed back his head, and did his best imitation of the screeching cry of a mountain lion. Even as he uttered it, he attacked.

The five Sioux war horses reacted predictably.

Whinnying and plunging in fright, they lit out across the basin for the far side. In their headlong flight they were not about to stop for anything or anyone, including the startled warriors who leaped erect in their path.

One of the warriors crumpled under flailing hooves. Another was struck head on by a gelding and sent sailing as if he were an ungainly bird. In their panic two of the horses ran through the fire, scattering burning brands every which way and raising a cloud of smoke.

Nate was right on their tails. A stumbling Oglala appeared in front of him and he swung the knife overhand, slamming the hilt onto the top of the man's head. The Lakota dropped like a rock.

From out of the smoke popped the Sioux wearing Nate's hat. Nate promptly hauled on the reins and rode him down. Then, vaulting to the ground, he sought his last foe.

It was the roper. The Oglala hurtled out of nowhere with all the feral fury of a berserk bobcat, his own knife flashing in a blur.

Pivoting, Nate countered a flurry of swings, their blades ringing together like chimes. The onslaught drove him backward, and he tripped over an unconscious Lakota. Unable to stop himself, he toppled.

The roper yipped and swooped in for the kill.

Flat on his back, Nate managed to get his right arm high enough to ward off the blow. Sparks seemed to fly from their knives. Again the Oglala came at him and he scrambled to the rear, barely staying out of reach as the warrior slashed down at him repeatedly. He couldn't keep it up forever, though. Inevitably, the Sioux would connect.

In order to buy time to regain his feet, Nate lashed out with both legs and caught the Lakota low on the shins. The man skipped to the left. Shoving into a crouch, Nate ducked under a wide strike, then leaped, the point of his knife aimed at the warrior's throat.

The roper was as agile as he was quick. Twisting and dodging, he evaded Nate and retaliated with a vicious stab below the belt.

More by accident than design, Nate parried and circled. The Lakota circled too, while around them fluttered wisps of smoke. One of the prone Sioux groaned. Nate feinted, chopped, spun and blocked. He was skilled at knife fighting, but the Oglala was his equal if not his better.

The fire had not gone out. Dancing flames cast their shadows on the surrounding slopes, resulting in a macabre shadow ballet.

Grunting, the Oglala flicked at the trapper's face, at his neck, at his midsection. Nate was hard pressed to stay one step ahead. Back-pedaling, he went on the defensive.

Then the roper did a strange thing; he reached behind him with his left hand. Darting in close, he cut at Nate's eyes. Instinctively, Nate brought his knife up to protect himself, and when he did, the Lakota's left arm reappeared. In the warrior's hand was the coiled rope, which darted out like the tongue of a serpent and looped around Nate's ankles. Before Nate could wrench loose, the rope tightened and his legs were yanked out from under him.

Instantly the Oglala pounced.

Winona King was riding toward Red Willow Creek in the dead of night when a peculiar tingle ran down her spine. It was as if an icy finger had stroked her from her head to her hips. She arched her back and looked around in consternation.

The air had not grown colder. The wind had not intensified. Winona had no explanation for the sensation.

Her people were ardent believers in omens and signs. From childhood she had been taught to look for the hand of the Great Mystery in all things. Which led her to hope that her odd feeling hadn't been a premonition of some sort.

Zachary King, attentive to his mother's every movement, immediately asked, "Are you all right, Ma?"

"Yes," Winona answered, hiding how disturbed she was.

"We should be there about the middle of the morning, don't you reckon?" Zach inquired. It had been her idea to head for Red Willow Creek, since that was where his father would expect to find them. He had wholeheartedly agreed in the hope it would see them reunited that much sooner.

There was a hitch, however. Now they were heading in the same direction the fleeing Crows and the Lakotas had gone. If the former had eluded the latter, they might encounter the returning Oglalas or stumble on their camp at any time.

So Zach rode with one hand always on his rifle and never lowered his eyes from the surrounding plain. He stayed close to his mother so if trouble did crop up, he would be right there to defend her and his sister.

Winona, on the other hand, entertained no worries about the Sioux. She was sure that she would hear them long before they spotted her. And, too, her mare was as reliable as a dog in that the animal would prick its ears at the sound of voices or other horses.

By traveling at night they reduced the risk. For

hours the prairie had been deceptively tranquil. So much so that Winona wanted to hold Blue Flower in her lap, but she needed to keep her hands free, just in case.

"Say, what's that?" Zach asked when a pinpoint of light flared in the distance. "A camp fire?"

"Yes. We must get closer," Winona said.

"It might be the Lakotas."

"It could be the Crows."

Unwillingly Zach let himself be guided in a horseshoe loop that brought them up on the site from the west. When they spied a number of figures hunched close to the fire, Winona reined up and whispered, "From here we go on foot."

"Why don't I go by myself?" Zach suggested. "One of us has to watch that the horses don't stray off, anyway."

Winona had to grin at his not so subtle tactic. "Our horses are well trained," she reminded him quietly. "We will stick together."

Neither of them were surprised to find that the warriors were Lakotas. Some were asleep, others swapping tales around the fire. Zach figured his mother would turn around once she had seen who they were, but to his astonishment she crawled closer. It seemed pointless to him until he saw the three bodies lying in a row.

Winona had spotted them from a long way off. Their identities were of no real consequence since they were beyond all help. But she had to know. Something deep within compelled her to get close enough to see their faces.

To do that, Winona had to skirt the camp to the north. Creeping along at the edge of the grass, she froze when one of the Oglala mounts raised its head and looked right at her. In her preoccupation with the corpses, she had forgotten that the wind would carry her scent toward the camp if she were not vigilant.

Zach imitated his mother. When a warrior glanced at the horses, he braced for a shout to ring out and expected to see the entire war party swarm toward them. The warrior didn't give the animals a second look, however, and turned back to his fellows. Presently the horse also lost interest.

Winona disregarded the tiny voice advising her to turn around before it was too late. Advancing, she soon saw the downturned face of one of the dead men.

It was Bear Ears. He had been stripped of all his clothes, so his wounds stood out like dark sores on his skin. In addition to the arrow that still jutted from his back, he had a large jagged hole in his side where a lance had sliced between his ribs. Where his throat had been was a gaping slit. And his scalp had been lifted.

Winona had to go farther to see the next Crow.

Runs Against had put up a terrific fight. Seven wounds marked his chest, several of them gashes left by knives or tomahawks. The fingers of his right hand were missing, as was his hair.

To go on invited discovery. Yet Winona couldn't stop herself. It was as if an invisible hand moved her along against her will.

The body nearest the fire was that of He Dog. Oddly, his clothes were still on him and there were no visible blood stains on them. Unlike the others, he was on his back, not his side, and his wrists were tied in front of him.

Winona assumed the Sioux had not yet gotten around to taking his scalp and whatever else struck their fancy, which in itself was unusual but not worth lingering over. Twisting, she signaled for her son to start back.

At that exact moment two of the Lakotas rose, walked over to He Dog, and jerked him off the ground. The Crow's eyes snapped wide. In blatant defiance he glowered at them.

"Goodness gracious! He's alive!" Zach whispered.

Winona could not believe it, either. She bore no affection for the man, but it bothered her to see him in the clutches of his merciless enemies. Far better for He Dog if he had died outright as Bear Ears and Runs Against did.

The Oglalas made the Crow kneel and then took turns heaping abuse on him. He was cuffed and kicked until he could barely hold himself up. A stocky Lakota drew a knife, seized He Dog by the hair, and jabbed the point under his skin at the hairline. The Lakota made a swift motion, as if he were slicing off the scalp, but he was only pretending. His friends laughed. He Dog endured their mirth stoically.

Winona had seen enough. It was time she got Stalking Coyote and Blue Flower out of there. Turning, she said to her son, "Lead the way. Remember not to move the grass."

"I know what to do," Zach declared, piqued that she would see fit to remind him. He wasn't a boy any longer. His parents had no call to remind him how to do things every chance they got.

Mother and son made slow progress. Many of the sleeping warriors had awakened, so now there were twice as many up as before. Some moved about, stretching their legs. As yet, none were near the west side of the camp, but that might change if one of them had to heed Nature's call.

Suddenly a roar of rage rent the night. An

Oglala had picked up a burning brand and applied it to He Dog's arm. The Crow caught them all off guard by lunging up off the ground and barreling into his tormentor. The Oglala staggered into the fire and let out a yelp. It elicited hearty laughter which changed to irate bellows when their captive spun on a heel and sprinted toward the high grass.

And toward Winona and her children.

Chapter Twelve

Nate King's legs were looped together by the Lakota's buffalo hide rope, but that did not prevent him from arching them to his chest and then ramming them outward.

The warrior was in midair, his knife arm cocked. Caught in the chest, he was catapulted onto the remains of the fire. Amid a shower of glowing embers and flaming limbs, he roared and bounded upright.

Rather than spend vital moments unwinding the rope, Nate severed it. He was almost to his knees when the Oglala came at him like a human whirlwind. The man's knife weaved a glittering web of gleaming steel which Nate barely parried.

The roper was beside himself. He took gambles no one with a shred of sense would take. Time and again he overextended himself or left himself wide open. Nate attempted to capitalize, but the man's lightning reflexes compensated for the mistakes.

The Lakota showed no signs of tiring. If anything, he appeared to be growing stronger. And wilder. Skipping out of reach of Nate's knife, he took one long step and leaped.

His blade streaked upward.

Nate was just starting to shift to the left. By a fluke, the warrior's stroke missed his torso and the man's arm came up under his own. Automatically Nate clamped his arm down, pinning the Oglala's at the wrist. The roper tugged, then clawed at Nate's neck with his other hand. It did not stop Nate from snapping his head forward and smashing his forehead onto the Sioux's nose. Warm blood spurted over them both. The Lakota jerked back but could go nowhere with his knife arm trapped.

It was the moment Nate had been waiting for. A short stab, and his blade sank to the hilt in his adversary's stomach. The Lakota stiffened and gurgled. Nate bunched his shoulder, twisted the knife, and sheared down and to the right, ripping the abdomen wide. As the Oglala sucked in a long breath, he swiftly retreated several steps.

The roper was in shock. He gaped down at himself and feebly attempted to stem the loss of his organs by placing both hands over the rupture. It was hopeless. Groaning, he sank to his knees. His knife fell to the grass. He looked up and spoke, his expression pleading.

The tongue was unfamiliar but the meaning was clear. Nate knew the warrior wanted to be put out of his misery. A belly wound like that was not always fatal right away. The Lakota might linger for hours in agony that defied belief. Nodding once, Nate moved closer. Executing an expert thrust to the heart, he did as the man wanted.

The Lakota closed his eyes and pitched over.

Suddenly something moved behind Nate. Whirling, he prepared to defend himself a second time, but the other four warriors were still unconscious.

Fetches Water had led the horses down into the basin. "I could not wait any longer, Grizzly Killer," she signed. Seeing the blood that speckled his features and clothes, she urgently added, "Are you hurt? I can tend your wound."

"I am fine," Nate wearily signed. The fight had taken a lot out of him, and he wanted nothing more than to curl into a ball and sleep for a week, but that was not meant to be. Hurrying from Lakota to Lakota, he retrieved his hat and pistol, as well as his ammo pouch and powder horn.

The girl helped herself to a knife and a bow. "I will not let them take me again," she explained.

Nate climbed onto the stallion. There was no trace of the horses he had driven off. With any luck, he mused, they either were on their way back to the village or had scattered to the four winds. It would take the better part of a day for the men he had knocked out to reach the Platte on foot.

Side by side, the pair trotted southward. Nate never relaxed his guard, and it was well he didn't. About two hours after the clash, a large knot of riders hove into sight to the west. Nate and Fetches Water reined up and held their breaths in anxious anticipation. The band was heading to the northeast. The warriors must have passed within 70 feet but failed to spot them.

The moment the hoofbeats faded, Nate went on. His companion impressed him with her composure. For one so young, she had all the qualities of a mature woman. And she was lovely. Small wonder that He Dog fancied her.

Dawn found them well over halfway to the area

where Nate expected to find his family and the Crows. He debated whether to lay low until sunset and elected to forge on. The sooner he reunited the girl with her father, the safer she would be.

Fetches Water agreed. Her fatigue showed, but she did not give in to it.

Twice before noon, bands of Lakotas appeared in the distance.

In the first instance, Nate promptly dismounted and made both horses lie down. While the girl held her hands over the pinto's muzzle, he did the same with the stallion.

The band contained nine warriors strung out in single file, bearing northward. They never came near enough to spot the trapper or Fetches Water.

The second instance was a closer call. Again Nate resorted to his trick of having their mounts lay in the grass. Pistol in hand, he watched as the band drew within 30 feet of their position. A heated discussion occupied the Lakotas, otherwise they would have seen him and the girl for certain.

Toward evening a belt of trees reared above the prairie like an island in the middle of a vast ocean. The belt widened, becoming a telltale band of lush vegetation of the sort that always flanked waterways.

Presently the horses were slaking their thirst at a bubbling creek while Nate scoured the nearby woods. In a small clearing he discovered the remains of a fire, which he pegged as no more than three or four days old.

Plenty of tracks had been left, and Nate was bending to inspect them when he heard something that sent him flying back toward the creek with his pistol drawn and cocked.

Fetches Water had uttered a shrill cry.

*   *   *

Winona King was rooted in place by the unforeseen sight of He Dog sprinting for his very life toward her and her children. They dared not leap erect and flee, or the Lakotas would see them. Yet if they just laid there, the Crow was bound to trip over one or the other and give their presence away.

"What do we do?" Zach hissed in alarm. There were so many Oglalas, they would be overwhelmed in moments if they were spotted. He might be able to drop one or two—before the rest were on them like a pack of ravenous wolves.

"Roll out of his way," Winona proposed, "and hope they do not notice the grass move."

He Dog was almost there. The beating he had suffered had taken a toll and he slowed, wheezing in pain. It was a mistake. Four fleet Sioux had given chase and were almost upon him. Hearing them, the Crow turned like a bull at bay and shrieked a challenge. They laughed, believing him to be helpless with his arms bound. They were wrong.

No one who knew him would ever deny that He Dog had many faults. But cowardice was not among them. Lowering his head, he charged the foremost Lakota and bowled the man over. He Dog spun and kicked another in the knee. The crack of bone must have been music to his ears, because he howled with glee and hurled himself at a third opponent.

This Sioux was more savvy. Dropping flat, he whipped his legs into the Crow's, upending He Dog, who landed hard on his shoulders. Before the Crow could rise, two of his enemies were on him. Try as they might, they couldn't pin his shoulders or legs. He Dog kicked and butted them with his head, knocking one man over and bloodying the other's mouth.

More Lakotas streamed from the fire. The Crow didn't stand a chance. He was buried under a half-dozen flying forms. A swirling melee broke out, attended by grunts and sharp cries and yelps of pain.

Then the warrior with the broken knee lurched upright, his features contorted in rage. He glared at the tangle of flying arms and legs while slowly drawing his long knife.

Winona knew what was going to happen next, but she was powerless to stop it. If she shot the Lakota with the rifle, the rest would be on her and her children before they took two steps. Clutching the Hawken in impotent dismay, she watched the inevitable outcome.

He Dog had still not given up. He thrashed. He snapped his legs right and left. He heaved his broad shoulders.

The warrior with the broken knee was watching intently, waiting for an instant when the press of bodies parted and he could see the Crow clearly. Suddenly that instant arrived. He Dog had shaken three men off his chest and was struggling to stand. In a flash the Oglala struck, lancing his blade into the Crow just under the sternum.

He Dog never uttered a sound. His body deflated like a punctured water skin and he melted to the ground.

One of the warriors checked and confirmed that the Crow was dead. It sparked an argument between the man who had killed him and several of the others, who apparently had wanted to take He Dog on to their village.

Winona wished they would go back to the fire. The nearest ones were less than ten feet away, and she feared they would glimpse Stalking Coyote or her if they turned toward the grass. Her heartbeat quickened when a burly specimen wearing eagle feathers did just that. He shifted and peered into the dark with narrowed eyes as if he sensed that he was being watched.

Winona's whole body broke out in goosebumps. She did not move a muscle, not even to blink. The Lakota scanned the grass and took a half step forward.

Just at that juncture, Evelyn squirmed. Winona felt her back move as the child shifted in the cradleboard. Should Evelyn cry out or so much as coo, the Sioux would hear her.

The burly warrior took another pace. He might have taken more except that a companion called out to him. The burly one hesitated a few moments, then gave a toss of his shoulders and rejoined his fellows. He helped tote the body.

Winona lost no time. The second their backs were to the grass, she snaked to the rear, whispering, "Quickly, son. To the horses."

Zach needed no prompting. His heart had about leaped into his mouth when the Lakota came toward them. He had been dead certain his days on earth were over, and he had been set to sell his life dearly. His belly scraping the ground, he crawled on his mother's heels.

They moved swiftly, Winona spurred on by an inner urgency, a foreboding that unless they got out of there something terrible would happen. And it did. At the selfsame second she laid eyes on the silhouettes of their horses, her daughter did the unthinkable: Blue Flower cried out in her sleep, a short, high-pitched wail.

From the camp rose an answering shout. At least one of the Lakotas had heard.

Throwing caution aside, Winona rose and ran. Her son could have gone on ahead, but he did not leave her side and did not mount his horse until she had mounted hers.

More yells issued from the camp. Figures were moving into the grass. One was on horseback.

"Ride!" Winona said, and did so, flying southward, gouging her horse with the stock of the Hawken to get it to go faster.

Young Zach glanced back. Several of the warriors had seen them and were gesturing excitedly. Soon the entire war party would be in pursuit.

The Sioux who was already astride a horse whooped and gave chase, waving his lance overhead.

Zach looked at his mother, then at the Sioux. On purpose, he slowed, keeping his mother in sight but allowing the warrior to gain on him. The man was 60 feet off. Then 40. At 30 feet, Zach sighted down his rifle. At 20 feet, as the warrior threw back his arm, Zach King fired.

The shot flipped the Lakota from his steed as the booming retort rolled off across the plain.

Winona twisted in surprise. She slowed until her son caught up, and chided half-heartedly, "You should have told me what you were going to do."

"No time," Zach said. "I couldn't let him get close enough to hurt you or sissy."

Her chest swelling with affection, Winona buckled down to the task of outdistancing the Oglalas. Their horses were tired but flowed smoothly across the prairie. When the sounds of pursuit grew in volume, she altered course to the southwest.

Zach could no longer see the Lakotas. He laughed lightly at their narrow escape, thinking of the tale he would get to tell his Shoshone friends. It would make them green with envy.

All of a sudden the grass thinned and before them lay a long stretch dotted with low dirt mounds. Winona realized the peril first and called out, "Prairie dog dens!" She jerked on the reins and swung to the left to go around the colony.

So did Zach. But as his horse began to turn, one of its front legs stepped into a dark hole. The resulting snap resembled the breaking of a large dry branch. A wavering whinny issued from the animal's throat as it pitched into a roll. Zach saw the ground sweeping up to meet him and frantically dived to the right so he wouldn't be crushed. A flying leg hit him in the side, jarring the breath from his lungs. He barely heard the tremendous crash nor a second louder snap.

Winona reined up and sprang to the ground before her horse came to a complete stop. She dashed back to her son, kneeling as he tried to sit up. "Be still," she cautioned. "You might have broken bones."

Zach let her probe to her heart's content while his swimming senses returned to normal. His vision cleared and he saw the stricken horse on its side, wheezing as blood gushed from its open mouth. The left front leg looked as if someone had taken an iron mallet to it and pulverized the bone.

"Can you stand?" Winona asked. He appeared to be unhurt, but she had known warriors who took spills and were never the same in the head again.

"I'm fine," Zach said. His mother helped him stand, regardless. He took a few tentative steps. Other than a throbbing bruise on his arm and a pulled muscle in his calf, he felt fit. Nodding at the horse, he said, "What do we do about him?"

The humane thing to do was put the animal out of its misery. But a gunshot would give them away to the Lakotas. Winona started to draw her knife. "We must do it quietly," she said.

"Let me, Ma." Zach moved in front of her and hunkered. The horse looked up at him with wide, anguished eyes. "I'm sorry, fella," he said softly. "I tried to avoid the darn burrows." His blade could split a hair; slitting the horse's throat posed no problem.

Now they had to ride double. Zach swung up behind his mother and was face to face with Evelyn, who grinned in impish glee. He held onto the sides of the cradleboard as they bore to the south, well shy of the prairie dog colony.

Winona did not let on that she was greatly concerned. The extra weight would tire the horse quickly, calling for frequent stops to rest. And if the Sioux caught sight of them, they couldn't possibly outrun those swift war horses.

Long into the night the pair put mile after mile behind them. At dawn they halted, but only briefly. Winona fed her daughter, Zach stretched his legs, then off they rode.

"We will keep going until we reach Red Willow Creek," the Shoshone declared. "There, we can hide and decide what to do next."

Morning gave way to afternoon. The day was hot and their horse plodded wearily along. Winona stifled yawns and occasionally shook herself to stay awake. Her daughter was asleep, and Zach had his eyes closed and was propped against the cradleboard when pinwheeling black dots high in the sky drew Winona's interest.

The dots were birds. Big birds. Presently Winona discerned that they were buzzards circling above their next meal. The scavengers of the wild were as common as buffalo, and she had no interest in going to investigate until she saw a chestnut horse all by itself, grazing near where one of the birds landed.

Letting her son sleep on, Winona made for the spot. The chestnut heard them and looked up but did not run off.

Eight or nine buzzards were clustered on a body. The only part of the man not covered by the big ugly creatures was his feet. The scavengers grew restless as Winona approached. A few squawked at her in irate annoyance for interrupting their gory repast. Winona simply ignored them.

One of the birds took a few awkward steps and launched itself into the air, its great wings flapping loudly. It was the signal for the rest to do the same. Not a single buzzard remained when Winona drew rein.

Yellow Owl lay on his back, his arms outstretched. He had been dead for quite some time. From his left side protruded an arrow. The angle suggested that he had turned to look at the pursuing Lakotas and been struck under his arm. Apparently he'd been able to keep on riding and had eluded the Sioux, but eventually the wound had proven fatal.

The buzzards had been thorough. The Crow's eyes, nose and ears were gone, as were both lips and his tongue. His stomach had been sheared open, and his intestines hung in partial loops. The fleshy parts of his shoulders and thigh had also been consumed. In some places, bone gleamed through.

Winona did not care for her children to see the grisly remains, so she went on. But someone already had.

"I hope to high heaven I never end up like him," Zach commented. "I can't stand the thought of those varmints pecking away at my innards."

"They serve a purpose, like everything else," Winona reminded him.

"I reckon so, but picking bones clean of rotten flesh isn't a purpose I'd go bragging on."

Winona had to laugh.

"I suppose He Dog and those other two are buzzard bait by now, too," Zach said. Picturing them being eaten made him queasy.

"I would say so, yes."

Zach recalled the terrific fight He Dog had put up. "You know, Ma," he said, "I never did like that contrary Crow very much, but if anyone asked, I'd have to say he went out like a warrior should."

"He was a credit to his people," Winona concurred, and meant it. She had been raised to believe that a man's worth was measured by his courage, and there could be no doubt that He Dog had shown his inherent bravery at the end.

For the rest of the day and into the gathering twilight, the Shoshone woman pushed their mount. When, at long last, she beheld the trees bordering Red Willow Creek, she brought the horse to a canter.

The woods were quiet when they arrived. At first Winona did not take note of it. She sat on a log and satisfied Blue Flower's hunger while Stalking Coyote took their mount to drink. Only when she was sitting there, slumped in fatigue, and had time to think, did Winona realize it was eerily silent. Birds should have been singing. Insects should have been buzzing and flitting about.

At the edge of the water, Zach saw his mother stiffen. With a start, he divined why. He brought his rifle to bear, scouring the vegetation for hostiles or beasts.

Deep in the brush, something moved. A shadowy figure appeared, then another, and two more.

Winona leaped up and spun to confront them. Zach ran over next to her, whispering, "More Lakotas, Ma! It has to be!"

But the boy was wrong. Smiling broadly, into the open walked Nate King. His wife and son took one look and were in his arms, hugging him close, too choked with emotion to speak. "About time the three of you showed up," Nate said in mock gruffness. "We were about to set out and find you."

"We?" Winona repeated, moisture rimming her eyes.

From the cottonwoods emerged Two Humps and Flying Hawk. Behind them came Bull Standing With Cow, his arm around the shoulders of a pretty young girl.

"Fetches Water?" Winona exclaimed, and when her husband nodded, she said, "But how?"

Nate escorted his loved ones to the clearing. They talked on and on, sharing their experiences. Winona and Zach laughed when he told how he had flown to Fetches Water after hearing her shriek, only to find her in the arms of her father.

The Crows were saddened to hear of the deaths of their four friends. Bull Standing With Cow pledged to help the families of the slain men as best he could.

"As for you, Grizzly Killer," the grateful father addressed Nate, "I will never forget what you have done for me. From this day on, we are brothers. Whatever is mine is also yours, and if I can ever help you, just ask."

Earlier that day, Flying Hawk had dropped a buck. Ample meat was left over, so Winona and

Zach helped themselves, the boy wolfing large gulps.

Shy of midnight, the Crows turned in. Nate and Winona strolled to the creek bank to be by themselves. The trapper placed his hands on her hips and drew her close, then paused as her lips were about to touch his. Their son had walked up. "Something wrong?" Nate inquired.

"I was just wondering," Zach said with an air of innocence they knew only too well.

"About what?"

"This summer. I think it would be nice if we spent some time with the Crows."

Father and mother exchanged knowing looks. "any special reason?" Nate probed.

Zachary King, otherwise known as Stalking Coyote of the Shoshones, gazed with a rosy gleam in his eyes at the sleeping form of the beautiful Absaroka girl by the fire and said with a straight face, "No. Not really."

#45
WILDERNESS
IN CRUEL CLUTCHES
David Thompson

Zach King, son of legendary mountain man Nate King, is at home in the harshest terrain of the Rockies. But nothing can prepare him for the perils of civilization. Locked in a deadly game of cat-and-mouse with his sister's kidnapper, Zach wends his way through the streets of New Orleans like the seasoned hunter he is. Yet this is not the wild, and the trappings of society offer his prey only more places to hide. Dodging fists, knives, bullets and even jail, Zach will have to adjust to his new territory quickly—his sister's life depends on it.

Dorchester Publishing Co., Inc.
P.O. Box 6640   ___5458-2
Wayne, PA 19087-8640 $5.99 US/$7.99 CAN

Please add $2.50 for shipping and handling for the first book and $.75 for each additional book.
NY and PA residents, add appropriate sales tax. No cash, stamps, or CODs. Canadian orders require
an extra $2.00 for shipping and handling and must be paid in U.S. dollars. Prices and availability
subject to change. **Payment must accompany all orders.**

Name: _____

Address: _____

City: _____ State: _____ Zip: _____

E-mail: _____

I have enclosed $_____ in payment for the checked book(s).

CHECK OUT OUR WEBSITE! *www.dorchesterpub.com*
_____ *Please send me a free catalog.*

LOREN ZANE GREY
AMBUSH FOR LASSITER

Framed for a murder they didn't commit, Lassiter and his best pal Borling are looking at twenty-five years of hard time in the most notorious prison of the West. In a daring move, they make a break for freedom—only to be double-crossed at the last minute. Lassiter ends up in solitary confinement, but Borling takes a bullet to the back. When at last Lassiter makes it out, there's only one thing on his mind: vengeance.

RIDERS TO MOON ROCK

ANDREW J. FENADY

Like the stony peak of Moon Rock, Shannon knew what it was to be beaten by the elements yet stand tall and proud despite numerous storms. Shannon never quite fit in with the rest of the world. First raised by Kiowas and then taken in by a wealthy rancher, he found himself rejected by society time after time. Everything he ever wanted was always just out of his grasp, kept away by those who resented his upbringing and feared his ambition. But Shannon is determined to wait out his enemies and take what is rightfully his—no matter what the cost.
